SOULS OF RESILIENCE

A CHRONICLE OF REAL WARRIORS...

FEBI ABRAHAM

Made with ♥ on the Notion Press Platform
www.notionpress.com

I dedicate this book to all the warriors in this world ,who are survivers of the bed of thorns, who have fought strong for their rights and principles of life.

Contents

Contents

Foreword

It is with delight that I write this foreword for *Souls of Resilience-A Chronicle of Real Warriors*, a magnificent collection of short stories written by Febi, my good friend and former colleague and HoD at the Department of English, Rajagiri Viswajyothi College of Arts and Applied Sciences. This book is a treasure that goes beyond storytelling, and dives deep into the depths of human emotions and its indestructible spirit.

Each story within these pages draws its content from the tapestry of real-life incidents, masterfully interwoven with the artistry of Febi's words. These tales, even though providing a feeling of being deeply personal, resonate universally, offering readers a mirror to their own lives or experiences of someone they know. While showing the struggles, triumphs and quiet moments of reflection portrayed, this book becomes a testament to the human spirit's ability to rise like a phoenix, time and again.

The ability to inspire without preaching can be seen with the skill to ignite a spark of courage in the hearts of the readers. With a language that flows effortlessly and a style that grips you from the first page, Febi as the author, invites us to embark on a journey of introspection and motivation.

In a world often marred by fear and regret, *Souls of Resilience-A Chronicle of Real Warriors* serves as a gentle yet powerful reminder to embrace life with courage, to cherish every moment, and to move forward unshackled by the past. It is more than a collection of stories - it is a guide, a companion, and a beacon of hope for each and anyone navigating the complexities of life.

May this book touch hearts, inspire minds and leave a fine mark on all the book-lovers who have the privilege of reading it.

Preface

It is okay to fall, but all that matters is whether you get up, dust yourself and move on!

How better can I describe this story collection briefly than this...! '*Souls of Resilience- A Chronicle of Real Warriors*' is a collection of short stories that are mostly based on real incidents woven in the fabric of words. The book will ignite in you a phoenix that will inspire you never to give up in life and to always move on without fear or regret.

Acknowledgements

I thank God, the Almighty for all the experiences of my life, and for all the people I have encountered in my life, whose stories have inspired me to write these stories. I thank my mother, Ms. Lali Joseph for her constant support as the Pole star in my life. I thank my husband, Mr. Justin Vallanattu Tom, for being the greatest support system that I can ever have. How can I forget to mention my son, Juan Joseph Justin, who was a part of me throughout the writing of this book during my first pregnancy. I also thank Dr. Tennyson Thomas, for editing and proofreading the book. My sincere thanks to all the readers, who trusted my writing skills and have purchased this book.

Prologue

There was a time, an era when the people who fall were judged and failures were nightmares...

But in the coming era, you won't be judged for your fall, but for not getting up...

So why waiting...Read on and move on...!

CHAPTER ONE

BREAKING THE CHAINS

Parenting in itself is a great learning process, the best way of which can never be determined. It is different for each child, no matter how many children you beget. A mother has a great role in the growth and development of her children. She is the root of the nurturing process. But what about the mothers who work abroad to be the backbone of the family, even though they have no idea how they are surviving each day.

Jhuria Bhutta, belonging to the Chamar caste of Uttar Pradesh, currently works as a nanny to the employer's kids in Saudi Arabia. Many of you may not be familiar when you hear the word 'chamarin'; it means she is belonging to the Chamar caste. She belongs to a Dalit community and Chamar people mostly do the job of tanning leather. They are among the castes formerly called untouchables. The Supreme Court order that calling a Scheduled caste as 'chamarin' is in itself an offence proves their status in the society. Their settlements are outside the higher-caste Hindu villages. Each settlement has its own headman known as Pradhan. She was a widow, but in the Chamar caste, a widow can marry her husband's younger brother. Her late husband left her with many debts and two children, a son and a daughter. Her present husband is not capable of doing any work other than the traditional leather work. It was at that time the Pradhan of their settlement brought forward this job offer, which he came to know from one of his acquaintances. The job was to be a nanny to the five children of a Sheikh in Saudi Arabia. Since she had a Diploma in Home Nursing, she was chosen. But it was just one month since she gave birth to her baby girl out of her present husband. She was not willing to go, but everyone in the family forced her to go, as that was the only way she could save the family from debts.

Her mother-in-law wanted her to work abroad and earn money to pay off the debts, and therefore her mother-in-law said that she would take care of the children. Jhuria taught her mother-in-law how to make the formula milk for the baby. She bought Nan-Excellapro powder and sterilized the bottle by boiling it in the hot water. She took one Oz of boiled water and added four spoons of Nan powder and shook it well. She asked her to keep the bottle in normal water till it reaches the room temperature. Till the two days before her flight, she fed her baby with her breast milk and the last two days she made her mother-in-law feed her child with the formula milk. She taught her everything, even to let few drops fall on her fist to make sure of the temperature of the formula milk.

Those last two days, before her flight Jhuria did not feed her baby girl, and she had to squeeze off the breast milk. It was disheartening to do that when her baby was crying for it, but if she gave her milk, what if she refuses to drink the formula milk after she left? In the beginning, the baby was reluctant, but by the time Jhuria left, she was feeding on it well. Just before she left for airport, Jhuria squeezed off her breast milk and she kept cotton clothes inside her brassieres to avoid wetting of her clothes throughout the journey. Jhuria held her baby girl close to her heart and wept. In that one month, she hardly got enough time to spend with her elder children, and they wept so bad hugging her tight when she left. Jhuria felt guilty of not being able to care for them much, and as she went in the rickshaw to the airport, she saw them standing still, so lost.

That was the first time Jhuria travelled in an airplane. She knew nothing, but one of the ground staffs helped her out. When she reached Saudi, she saw her name on a placard, and thus she was taken to the Sheikh's house. One cannot even compare the facilities that one gets in Saudi with what one gets in one's homeland. Everything about the system of Gulf countries was that perfect. The Sheikh's wife welcomed Jhuria and took her to her room. As she was walking to her room, Jhuria fell unconscious. The family doctor came and said it was just because her blood pressure was high, and probably because she was missing her children. They were good people; they let her take rest that whole day. The next day, Jhuria felt better and she was introduced to the five children; the eldest one was ten years old and the youngest one was just one month old, just like her baby.

The eldest one was named Azzam, a very naughty boy of the same age as Jhuria's son. The middle child was a sweet little girl named Raziya. She was special to Jhuria as she was about the same age of her second daughter. The one-month-old child was named Zaira. It was not that she was partial to those kids or that she doesn't care about the other two children, it was just that those three children reminded Jhuria of her own kids. The first job she did in that house was to give a bath to Zaira baby. As she was giving her bath, tears started rolling down as she remembered her youngest one who was as tiny as Zaira baby.

Jhuria was always with Zaira baby. When Madam was sick and she couldn't breast feed, Jhuria was asked to lactate Zaira baby. She was feeding her employer's child with her breast milk, whereas her own baby was feeding on the formula milk. Jhuria saw Zaira's first steps, and Zaira calling her mother 'Ammi' for the first time. From her salary, Jhuria sent her husband money to buy a smart phone. At least she could see her children, but she missed her own baby's first steps and her first utterance. Jhuria's husband said he was away for work when their baby took her first steps. It was Jhuria's mother-in-law who told him the same when he returned from work. Almost all the time that Jhuria made a call to home, the baby would be sleeping. Jhuria only got to talk to her elder children. If at all the baby was awake, she either ignored to give Jhuria a look or went on crying. It was so disheartening. Jhuria really wished she smiled at her when she called her, but she was just a stranger to the baby, a total stranger. Another day, she got the good news that her baby made her first utterance. Instead of saying 'Maa', she uttered 'Baba'. She didn't know if she should be happy or be sad. This is how life treats you when you are away from your baby. Jhuria know well that she needs her, but what about living a life doomed in debts, and what about the future of her children! These realizations were what that helped her go on.

One day, when Jhuria made a call to home, as she was talking to her eldest son, her second daughter fell. Neither her husband nor her mother-in-law cared to attend her. Her daughter was going on crying lying on the floor. Jhuria did everything she could to console her. She wished her hands could hug the child close to her heart. That day she was there on phone, but what about other days? That thought left her heart trembling.

Another day, when Jhuria called, she sensed that her son was looking different. She felt there was something that he was hiding from her, that he was keeping to himself. No matter how many times she repeatedly asked he did not say anything. When Jhuria talked to her daughter, she took the phone and went outside. She told Jhuria how he was forced to work with his step-father, and how he was forced to learn the trade. He was also made to do difficult works like carrying big logs. She told how he never got time to study, but still he got the second position in the class, and how no one from the family attended his felicitation program. That hurt him the most. He doesn't talk like how he did before; he always remained silent making charcoal paintings. When Jhuria saw his paintings, it clearly showed the depressive state of his mind and his insecurity. Her daughter also told her how they were planning to stop her schooling. She was made to do all the household chores. Many a times, her hands got burnt. There were burnt marks all over her arms.

Jhuria was terribly sad to see the pitiful condition of her elder children. The youngest one was not liked well as she was a girl child.

Her husband and his mother longed for a boy baby to be their heir, and her husband was not ready to see Jhuria's eldest son as his heir. They are also the same blood. Jhuria fought with her husband and her mother-in-law. They didn't seem to care at all, and was asking money for the monthly expenses. All they cared for was her money!

Jhuria used to see how her employers took care of their kids. They invited even her for their eldest son's felicitation programme for getting the tenth rank in the school, and in India. Jhuria's son got second rank and no one went to take part. Sitting there among the audience, how happy the employer's boy was receiving the prize and he was waving at his family. Jhuria could feel how bad her son must have felt when no one turned up to appreciate him. Jhuria understood that she can never make her family members value her children, it is their choice but she can; she can value them. She can give them the care that they deserve. That day, that felicitation day of her employer's child, she took the decision to quit her job and be the mother that her children deserve. After all, she was earning for her children's better future and what was the use of her earnings when her own children are deprived of their rights and falling into a depressed state?

Jhuria's employers understood her concern and allowed her to leave. Her family was never happy. They kept on scorning at her, but she knew what was right. They scorn her even now; but she doesn't care anymore. Children need a loving and supporting atmosphere. The world in which they grow up and the attitudes of people who surround them are very important in the growth and nurturing of a child. Parents need to spend quality time for their children. Only the involvement and the presence of the parents can be a solution to the disconnections. Jhuria's eldest son was in that state and she wanted him to know that even if no one cares, she cares!

When she was working abroad, the time difference mattered a lot too. She had to be on service even at night and was not getting time to call. That was the main reason for her to quit that job. The only consolation that her children had was her phone call. If she can't even call them, she doesn't think her job is an ideal one for her. People in their locality keep asking her when she is returning for her job. When she told them that she is not returning they reacted as though she was doing a sin. They often ask her if her decision was a wise one. Her answer is always, 'Yes'.

CHAPTER TWO

LIVING WITH GRACE

Life is a mystic journey; a journey that surpasses vistas of happiness and streams of sadness. The trails of happiness can take you into an aura of a make belief world whereas the string of sadness is enough to drown you into an eye-opening despair. Ritu's life was also a roller-coaster ride of joy and sorrow.

Ritu's husband was an ex-military person. Her children, her daughter and her son were born and brought up in Mumbai. Ritu was a beautician by profession. Her daughter being so pretty had won many beauty pageants and her son was an expert basketball player. Once her son finished his high school, they decided to move back to Kerala.

Moving back to Kerala was a varied experience. Being exposed to a very broad-minded cosmopolitan life for past twenty-five years, one would definitely find it hard to sustain in a narrow-minded countryside. The necessary intruding and inquisitive nature of the people was what that irritated them the most, especially their children. People had problem with them in everything, from the dressing of her daughter to the grill that they fitted around their house. But they had to cope up with that, as her husband wanted to live in the land where he was born and brought up. East or west, home is the best, was after all his regular saying.

Whatever the society felt, they were living a happy and contented life. Her daughter completed her B.Ed. course and her son joined B.Sc. Nursing after his higher secondary. When her son entered the second year of Nursing, her daughter got married. She had fallen in love with a Tamil Christian and they happily married her off. Her marriage became the main matter of gossip in their locality for many months. People criticized them and blamed that they were dancing to the tunes of their children. They even degraded her for having a love marriage and for marrying a Tamil guy. She and her husband always did seek to let their children live as they wish, provided it was not anything that mean.

It was as though her husband was waiting for their daughter's marriage that he suddenly passed away after a month due to a silent heart attack. It was such a hard time for Ritu, but she knew that he went happily fulfilling all his duties towards their children. He had saved enough for their son's studies and had kept aside some money in her name. Only after he passed away, she knew this, and her eyes welled up thinking how thoughtful he was.

During her son's final year, she was called to her son's college and was informed that her son impregnated one of his classmates; the girl was said to be his lover. Luckily, it was during the probation period and they quickly arranged his wedding. He had no money to start his new life and she therefore gave him whatever money her husband had set aside for her. With that, they managed their expenses till he got a job. It was hard for him and he was helplessly dependent on Ritu. One after the other, most of my gold was pawned. One after the other, she got three baby girls in five years. All of them were born within a short gap of time. His mother-in-law mostly stayed with them, which led to a great influence of her on Ritu's son. He was more available to her family than he was to Ritu. Sometimes she went and stayed, but she often felt she was not as welcome as she was supposed to be.

Since she felt some sort of indifference at her son's home, she chose to live at her husband's home itself. Since her daughter lived with her in-laws at Chennai, Ritu hardly went there to stay. If at all she went, it was but just as a visit. As she was staying on alone, her daughter-in-law informed Ritu that her mother passed away. She was deeply bereaving and she requested Ritu to come and stay with them. Her son and daughter-in-law lived a luxurious life, spending so much money on parties, movies and dining out. They never took Ritu along with them and she never complained. It was during that time that her son went to Canada looking for a job. After he left, the attitude of her daughter-in-law started changing completely. She started talking back to Ritu, used to get irritated soon, and always remained in their room with the kids. Ritu remained doing all household chores by herself.

Occasionally, her daughter-in-law made some delicacies, but she would take it directly to the room and never gave Ritu a single piece to taste. One such day, Ritu felt some pain around her breasts, and she told her daughter-in-law but she ignored. Ritu bore the pain for six months but in six months the pain increased, and she shared it to her daughter. Upon her daughter's call, her daughter-in-law took Ritu to an oncologist. Mammograms were done and Ritu was recommended to do a biopsy. Doctors were genuine and they chose not to fake it. She was diagnosed with stage two, breast cancer. The moment was so dark that she felt the entire world stopped in that moment. She felt she skipped a few heart-beats. Ritu was sad; anger filled her thinking how it could happen to her! Her cancer had started spreading to her lymph nodes. Surgery and chemotherapy were recommended. But they had no money.

That day itself, her daughter-in-law told at her face that Ritu cannot stay there anymore. She kicked Ritu out of the house with no mercy. She returned to her home.

When her daughter came to know about it, she was terribly upset. She called her brother and shouted at him for ill-treating their mother. She asked Ritu to come and stay with her, but Ritu couldn't do it. Her daughter was with her in-laws and Ritu didn't want to be a burden.

Ritu's son had some financial liabilities and without even thinking about Ritu, he tried to sell their house where she stayed.

It was such an alarming and disheartening situation. Her daughter and son-in law received a stay from the court and saved Ritu from the situation. Meanwhile doctors told her that she must do her surgery at the earliest before the situation worsens. There were some teak trees in their land. As per her daughter's suggestion, they sold all the trees in their land and amassed enough money for her treatment. Unfortunately, her son was against selling those trees. He said that it was his property.

The pain that her son was causing her was worse than that of the cancer she had. Whenever she laid down, she wondered how he turned so heartless towards her. She decided that she should not be sitting and crying at her plight. She started training her mind to fight against all the negative thoughts that were lurking in her mind.

Her surgery was done following some chemotherapy treatments. Her hair fell and she started looking like a monster. A beautician turned into a monster! Doctors told her that she was freed from the threat of cancer and that she was cured completely from it. Earlier many a time she had questioned God how he could do this to her. She had asked if this was the reward for all the selfless community services that she had done. She even thought that God does this to those who are close to him, and she doubted should she have not been so religious to save herself from these tribulations.

Ritu believes that there is a reason for everything that happens in one's life. At least it helped her to open her eyes to the real nature of her son and daughter-in-law, whom she had valued more than her daughter, whom she had been blindly trusting. Certain pains save you from worse ones...

CHAPTER THREE

FEEBLE HANDS OF LOVE

The bond of the heart is the deepest one that one can ever have for a person. It is not always necessary that you find that bond only in your blood relations. A caring neighbour can serve as such a person.

When I was married and was introduced to my husband's house for the first time, amidst the many people who came to see me, there was this one person who wore a dhoti kind 'Kaili' and a white towel over the blouse. 'Kaili' is the dhoti kind attire the women of Kerala wore in the olden times and even now. As my eyes quickly passed from one end to the other, it got stuck on this fragile woman, so lean and wrinkled. The ceremonies got over, and the next day morning she was there at the door.

My mother-in-law introduced her as Ramani amma, our nearest neighbour. She was so happy to see me, her eyes twinkled with joy, and she started talking to me by addressing me as 'Ponnu'. And I loved being addressed as that, as so far in my life, I was addressed only by my name. As I was sweeping the courtyard, she was washing the clothes by beating the clothes on a rock used for washing clothes.

In the afternoon, when I came out of the kitchen, I saw my husband standing in front of her house, talking to her. What interested me was the little kitten which was jumping around in front of her house. There were other adult cats too. I slowly went there and sat on the dusty steps of her house. She was feeling ashamed that I sat there and also because she did not have a chair to make me sit. I was very comfortable and I assured her that I feel good to sit there. As the conversation began, she was so curious to know about the gold ornaments I had. I told her that not all that I wore on wedding day were real gold. Some were fancy ornaments and I added that my husband married me without asking dowry. I had heard that she had the habit of telling everyone, and I was sure that she would tell that too. I didn't feel the need of telling lies in any way.

Slowly the bond began. Whenever I cooked a curry, I gave her a portion of it. I still do that and she would also bring me what she cooked. Sometimes, I take her help in kitchen works as well to grate the banana flower or to clean small shrimps. I would give her a pocket money and she would be happy. She used to wash clothes near to our kitchen door and I always love to chit chat with Ramani Amma.

One thing that I like about her is that she cares for me as her own child. Whenever she comes calling me 'Ponnu', I feel so happy and loved. She had seen my husband as a child and therefore I respect her the same way as I respect his parents. When I travelled to Oman last time, she was there to bid me farewell, and as I took blessing from our elders by touching their feet, I did the same for her and I saw tears in her eyes as I left.

She is a woman who is deeply saddened by the deeds of her irresponsible sons who least cares to provide basic necessities of life for her. She is all the time worried for her children and grieves the ungratefulness, yet she is always doing everything for them and even at this ripe age, crossing 65, she walks down the hill to fetch drinking water, and throughout the day we can hear the rhythm of her washing the clothes by beating it thoroughly on the rock. My husband and I asked her to use our bore-well water for drinking purpose, but she chooses to walk down the hill and collect fresh running water from the stream. Meanwhile, she can talk to everyone on the way, and that in a way rejuvenates her mind. She continues to live so, having a family feeling for everyone she comes across...

CHAPTER FOUR

RISING FROM ASHES

Love is the most magical feeling that one can have; to be loved back is the greatest magic that can happen in one's life. Rianna never believed in love until she met him. It was during her graduation days. The day she felt for him for the first time, she wrote in her diary, "Rianna, you are in love!"

Rianna belonged to a family which was full of ardent lovers of the Congress party. Everyone in her family loved to watch the news rather than movies, including her. Their family was an unusual one. They had discussions after the dinner and family prayer. Usually, younger ones are not allowed to be a part of the discussions, but in her family, she always had my voice, right from her infancy. She had grown up hearing stories of the freedom struggle and independence. Stories of Mahatma Gandhi, Indira Gandhi and Rajeev Gandhi always inspired her to be a truly patriotic person. She was taught to stand in attention whenever she heard the National anthem. Not just Rianna, her entire family used to stand up and honour the National anthem whenever they heard it. When she grew up, she chose to be in a government college, because she loved the political activities and social activities that happen in such colleges.

She joined in a government college in Kottayam district, a majestic campus which had a good architectural brilliance in its infrastructure. College was good, and as they were enjoying their college days, the campus elections came up. The election campaign was going on.

One day, she was walking in the corridor, and the election campaign passed her. One of them happened to hit her by mistake, and her books fell. As she was taking the books, one hand stretched out to her and handed over a book. That was him! The one standing in the college election to be the Union Chairman! That was the first time she saw him.

Cladded in a white cotton shirt and dhoti, he smiled as he gave her book to her. She held her breath and she felt like she was in some other world. With that smile, he turned and walked away, followed by a trail of followers. What impressed her the most was his thoughtfulness to help her out, rather than acting like a boss. Everyone in her class liked him and shared many stories that they had about him from the seniors, mostly about the social outreach programs that he initiated in the college, in his first year of graduation itself.

She started observing him whenever she saw him. He was very kind and considerate towards others. He had no lust for power and he never tried to impress anyone. He had his own viewpoints about everything and never stepped back from standing up for what was right. He was always open to constructive criticisms. She was very sure that he would win; and she supposed that even his opponents were sure that he would win. Everyone in the campus loved and admired his persona, even she.

Once when she was standing outside her class, he passed by as he came to see their teachers. He stopped by her, looked at her and she was startled. He asked her, "Will you support me with the election campaign among the first years?" She was so taken aback that she just tilted her head to and from meaning 'yes'. From then, she was very active in campaigning for him in her batch. She loved to see him and gradually she started longing to see him. And when she saw him, she felt she was swooning off.

His success in the college elections was a great celebration. There was a reception for him and there was a performance by the drum artists of Kerala. All danced to the drumbeats and her dancing to the tunes of the drums went viral on social media. The other day, when he saw her, he said that her performance was superb. He also asked her support in all his activities. He brought many changes to the college. His first campaign was to turn the entire college into a plastic free campus. He took initiative in planting more trees which was a great step, taken towards making the campus a green campus. He then started the "One meal, one smile" campaign, where all those who are willing could donate one meal in the boxes kept there, which was distributed to the vagabonds during the lunch interval, on a daily basis.

What she loved about him was that he was not bossy by giving orders, but he worked along with others. He was often described as "the most promising leader of tomorrow". There were some against him; they threw cow dung on his poster. She felt so bad, and she went and removed it with her hand. He noticed it.

That evening, as Rianna was sitting in the canteen, he came and sat opposite to her. He said that there were rumours that she had a crush on him, and he asked her if that was true. She didn't look at him and she kept on fidgeting the five-rupee coin that was in her hand. He took it at once and asked her if she would like to join him in the roller-coaster journey of his life. She had a smile on her face and he said that he was taking it as her 'yes'. He said that his life was always unexpected, that he never thought if he would ever have a woman in his life, and that the lady in his life would be Rianna. She was sitting silent, but a DJ was playing in her mind; that was her first-hand experience of a proposal of love.

They were very much different from other couples. Unlike others, they didn't always meet up during the intervals. After the class, they met under the banyan tree and discussed whatever they wanted to. Sometimes when he had community services, they didn't meet. She understood him completely and supported him in all his ventures. Unlike the other couples, they hardly talked on phone. All her friends who had boyfriends were always on phone, chatting, calling for hours, and even video calling till they slept. He hated chatting and he was never a person who liked video calling. He would call once in a day before he slept. If he was late, he would call just for a minute and would ask her to go to sleep. But there was a depth of understanding that they had.

After he got graduated, he continued to call as usual. But in few months, he became the Secretary of the party and from then his priority was always the activities of the party. Calls reduced, and she could understand his situation, though she felt insecure. She started messaging him all the necessary information. For six months it continued like that and one day she saw his missed call. She was happy that he found time to call her, but when she called him back, he said his future is uncertain and that he didn't think he is meant for a family life. He asked her to move on. She told him that she can wait as long as he wanted, and he said that he had no hope of having a family life. His attitude to life had changed and he was sure about the decision that he had made.

In the beginning, she couldn't believe it was true; she couldn't believe it happened to her. She continued messaging him and calling him till the day he blocked her. That dejection wiped away the earth under her feet. She spent most of her time crying alone in her room. Her hostel mates tried their best to pacify her, but it was all in vain. It was in the month of October, and their college had rosary in the college chapel. Every day, she attended the rosary kneeling. It was at that time that they had the Literary Fest in the college. She was selected as one of the anchors. She took it as the first step to move on, but she terribly failed. In between the programme, she ran out and cried. She felt that she let down her classmates, her teachers and her department but since there was another anchor, the programme went on quite well. Those were crucial days of her life - the first phase of dejection.

Even though she tried to hide her emotions deep within herself, people around her, people who were close to her, started figuring out her broken self. She was thankful for all those kind words and warm hugs, because that helped patching up her wounds to a certain extent.

After post-graduation, many of her classmates joined various colleges for work, but her mind was like a floating boat with no radar. As she wanted to give a chance to her relationship, she joined the Civil Service coaching centre near her college. It was his dream to see herself as an IAS officer. Though his dejection left her a lost soul, his buried dreams about her became her patched wings.

Though she began her IAS coaching as her means to get him back, today it has become her own dream, a duty that she has towards the humanity. Even though some corner of her heart still longs for him to come back in her life, she has far surpassed the condition of being taken away by such thoughts. She is taken up by a mission in her life to be someone worthy in this society, of whom her parents can be proud of, someone whom she herself can look up to.

CHAPTER FIVE

PAGES OF LONELINESS

Often it is praised that marriages are made in heaven. But what if the heavens don't let you marry due to the astrological problems? Such is the story of Ardra and Dhwani.

I met Ardra and Dhwani in the paper valuation camps. Both of them were lecturers in self-financing colleges under the same university. In the valuation camps one becomes a part of a valuation team randomly. I was also part of their team.

As we were waiting for the answer scripts, our chief came and sat beside us. We were a team of three males and three females along with the chief. First day since the team was just formed, we had only 5 answer scripts to evaluate. That would not even give us enough money for our travelling expense, still we all come seeking the little additional income, other than the salary. You will find many young lecturers who look more like students and will end up wondering how many self-financing lecturers are there in the state. Many are there who are struggling with meagre salary and for them, the few thousands that they would receive matters a lot, and they come happily to such valuation camps. Perspectives change with situations.

Ardra and Dhwani seemed to be in their late 30's, but they said they were not married yet, in their introduction. I did not poke them with unnecessary questions. During the break time, it was told that if we give the order, the canteen staff would bring tea and banana fritters. I had heard from many that the biriyani served in the canteen was awesome, and I was waiting eagerly for it to be noon so that I could devour the biriyani. The rate of the biriyani and the travelling expenses did not meet with the day's earnings, but I didn't want to complicate myself with those calculations. After the day's work, while I was having my biriyani, Ardra and Dhwani came and sat beside me. They were having meals. While sprinkling the salt on the rice, Dhwani asked me if I was married and I nodded with a smile. Dhwani went on speaking about how her life is in disharmony because of the tensions regarding the people's inquisitive nature about her not getting married. I told her not to worry and that everything would fall in its place at the right time. Dhwani mentioned about the astrological issues because of which it is hard to find a suitable groom. When she said so, Ardra opened up and said that it was due to astrological reasons that her marriage was not taking place as well.

Dhwani's family was a conservative orthodox Hindu family. Her father passed away when she and her elder brother were at school. From then, their mother brought them up in a very strict and disciplined manner. Throughout her schooling and college life, Dhwani was in a girls only educational institution. So there was no chance of mingling with any boys at all. Even all her cousins were girls. Gradually, it became difficult for her to speak to the opposite gender other than her brother. It was just last year that her mother passed away, and by that time Dhwani was 38. She is living in a working women's hostel as her brother was living abroad. Even her brother was not married. She thinks it's because she is not married that her brother is not showing interest to get married. Dhwani said that she and her brother never bring that topic to discussion.

Ardra said that she was often humiliated by her relatives and was often taunted by some colleagues. For them it is a joke, but only those who undergoes the pain knows how it feels. Ardra was mentioning about a male staff who often mocks her for getting old and still not being married. The male staff was unmarried too and he was from another religion. Ardra was short-tempered and whenever she reacted back, he insulted her in front of everyone mocking that nine days a month Ardra would keep blasting referring to her periods. The male staff used to look at every lady in a dirty manner. She described how one day he was gazing at a senior lady teacher who used to sit next to her. His eyes would run a marathon race from the lady's eyes to breast again and again. It was so disgusting, but she had to continue working there as there was no other college that paid her better. As we completed our lunch, we paid our bill and walked to the entrance of that college to catch the bus to our own destinations.

That entire one week was eventful. Valuations and revaluations! Sometimes there will be compulsion not to give beyond a total mark whereas sometimes we would be forced to give a pass mark, and we did as we were instructed. On the last day of paper valuation, we shared our WhatsApp numbers and added each other as friends. From then, it has been two years that we had offline paper valuation. We used to keep in touch once a while. Recently, I saw on Facebook that Ardra got married. The groom was also a middle-aged man, but they looked so happy and content. I called Dhwani and she said she had no social media account, so she didn't know about it. We talked for a while and she told that for few months she was with her brother at her ancestral home as he came for his vacation. Now, she was packing her belongings to be back to her hostel once again. There was so much dryness in her voice and I could imagine her walking into uncertainty as I stood helpless at the other end of the phone...

CHAPTER SIX

DUTIFUL AND RIGHTEOUS

Childhood days are very special for everyone and after one age, the memories that give us the greatest nostalgia would be the memories of our childhood days. My mother always made me participate in almost all the competitions, especially Arts related competitions. When I was young, I lived in the school where my mother was working. She used to take me around for many speech competitions.

My mother used to train me on how to deliver a speech. She used to tell me to start the speech in a lower tone, and as the speech progresses, the tone should be higher, and towards the end, the tone should be lower. I was ready with the speech and I was taken to the venue. The competitions were of Catechism classes, a zonal competition.

As I reached that old school, there were not many people there. We were always early everywhere. Mummy was well set with everything - my speech with all the slashes at the pauses, water to drink and bread sandwiches which she made with jam and butter. As she was feeding me with it all, the crowd started increasing gradually. Every contestant from each church had a classroom to get dressed up and be ready for the competitions; there was also the dance master who was getting the hairdo and make up ready. I was sitting amidst them, like an Alice in Wonderland.

As I was taught, I delivered the speech well with all the body languages and voice modulations. I was more curious to go and watch the dances, but my mother was fond of listening to other speeches. I must have be in class 5 or 6. As I was loitering around the corridor, I saw my mother eagerly watching a boy's speech. To my surprise, the boy was delivering the speech just as how my mother taught me. He had the perfect voice modulation, so much energy and life, and he also started the speech at a low tone, raised it eventually, and reduced the tone at the end with an emotionally persuasive note. As we were leaving back to the school where we lived, I saw him roaring "*Jai Jai Parathanam*", an utterance that was usually done at that time whenever our parish won the trophy.

He was wearing a white shirt and black pants, probably his attire of his First Holy Communion. My mother was very fond of him for his eloquent speech and for the struggles he had to go through. As I grew up, I learnt that he was brought up by a single parent, his mother; just as I was brought up by my mother. Being born on the day of the assassination of Shri. Rajeev Gandhi, he was named Rajeev. From then, I felt a great admiration for the way that boy was having a great spirit.

Years passed by and I lost all the ties with everyone as I lived three years in Manipur for my graduation. When I returned, there were many new families and all those who were there during the Catechism days went different places for their further studies. Years later, I was grown up with more downs than ups in my life. As I was teaching in a prestigious college, during the lockdown period I had created many mini lectures which would be useful for my students. I had uploaded them first on Facebook and later on YouTube. One such day, I got a message from him, Rajeev. He told me that he is one of the owners of an international academy which is specialized in IELTS and OET. Seeing my mini- lectures, he invited me to be a trainer in his academy. After two years, when I moved to Salalah, I joined his academy. From then, I came to know more about him and how kind a gentleman he had become, with a fellow feeling for others.

What touched me deeply were his will-power and persistence. Even as a child, he must have gone through a lot for being raised up without a father, just like me. And that very fact about our similar childhood is what connects us today and the reason why he is like a brother to me than my boss. He left his career in banking field and did many startups. One after the other, he succeeded in every field. The way he treats his mother like a queen is worth a salute. All the pains of that mother got answered by God through a worthy son. Seeing many of his statuses on social media, one made me feel so much proud about him; it was a status where his mother was driving through a desert. That made me wonder what more can a mother want than a son who uplifts her, makes her independent and treats her like a queen. That is what I admire so much about him; the way he makes his mother live like a queen herself.

CHAPTER SEVEN

THE ART OF BALANCING

"Ambujam...Ambujam..."

Every day begins with this call of her mother-in-law.

"The water tanker has come. Go and get the water fast."

Ambujam would wake up fast, brush her teeth and uneasily roll up her hair to rush out with two plastic pots. Standing in the queue and having to listen to the chatter of neighbouring women was the most irritating part of her day. They keep on asking whether she was not trying for a second child as her son Shambu turned six years old. Sometimes she wonders why those women, who seem to be no one in her life, must bother about her own "personal" life! She would just scorn them in her mind and divert her contempt into a fake smile. With all the pushes and pulls, when she finally manages two pots of water, she would feel so exhausted, but it is so hard to realize that the day has just began!

The household chores start with sweeping the courtyard, making the 'kolam' with rice powder, helping her mother-in-law with cooking the breakfast and lunch on time. By any means, the tiffin must be ready on time. Meanwhile, she gets to hear 'Ambujam...' from the head of the family, her father-in-law who would be enquiring about his medicines. From the other end, her husband would be yelling "Ambi...where is my socks, my file, my spectacles etc.' As she would be reaching out to them, her son

Shambu would have his own tantrums. Waking him up to getting him ready for school before the school bus comes, is itself such an exhausting task. We women would always hide our pains in the little shadows of love...

After all, the rat race is the task to be at office on time. As she gets ready and rushes to the bus, her mother-in-law would say,

"Ambujam, why don't you put some powder on...at least some kajol...not even a bindi! And how carelessly have you draped your saree...your hair also not plaited properly."

She would give a smile, and as she rushes, she would hand some money to her so that she can buy fresh vegetables from nearby farm.

Ambujam's office work is not as simple as sitting on a chair and handling the accounts. Being the youngest of all, she was the one who mostly was bound to take up all the toughest dealings. Sometimes, not sometimes, many a time I must go to the Head Office to get signatures from the Managing Director. Her MD is very particular about getting the papers ready by the accounting staff itself rather than sending it off through a peon. There is no peon as well, so I am the one who always climbs up and climbs down the entire day! As she reaches back with a gasp, Kusumam Ammal would smile and say, "See this is Ambujam's trademark secret". In my mind she would wish to ask, "Why don't you have some portion of my 'trademark secret'?", but she would hide it again with a smile and would get back to her seat.

As the work gets more hectic, sometimes she must take her work to her home which she really hates. Well...the family members won't understand the situation, which is the first problem. Mother-in-law would think that the whole day she had to handle the child, and Ambujam herself must handle the child in the evening as well.

Children at such younger age need their mother the most. Her son Shambu is normally a manageable kid, but even he would long for her presence with him at least in the evenings. From his very young age, she was the one who used to teach him. So, he likes to do his homework only with Ambujam. His father doesn't know to deal with him in a soft manner, so Shambu feels more comfortable with her. Whenever she ponders on that, she feels that all of us are working for the future of our children and family, but if we are unable to spend time with our children, then what is the purpose of all the toiling done! This increases her feelings of futility and makes her feel guilty. But what if she doesn't work? She really cannot put all the pressure on her husband and let him bear it all.

Even though her mother-in-law helps her with the household chores, she needs to do most of the works. She is also not physically that well, yet she tries her best, mostly in soothing Shambu when he puts forth his tantrums. She got that magic in her and her stories as well as her tricks works well with Shambu as well.

Old age is second childhood. Parents often get sick, and they need to be taken care of as kids at times. Sometimes they can be fuzzy about little things and can get easily irritated. They may have mood swings as well. For a working woman, it is really a task to manage. Managing household expenses is yet another task. Everybody treats men as the bread winner, but only working women know how the little vegetables and grocery they buy on the way back home from work helps balancing the expenses! We cannot wait for the husband to bring everything, you know. Sometimes or many times they forget. When a tomato or a coconut is needed for a particular dish, it must be brought, right? When husbands forget, it flops "the entire plan of the day" actually. These are the things only women can understand.

Everything in life need not be bed of roses. Amidst all of these, there are also other aspects which can affect a working woman. If marital relationship is not running smoothly with proper understanding, it can be a pain in the neck! Even though physical relationship is a conjugal right, it may not be possible for a working woman to have it whenever the husband wants. Just imagine! The entire day, one is working starting with the household chores in the onset of the day and later at office, only to come back at home and continue the chores! Finally, when one feels like as though they are crawling to reach the bed to have a sound sleep, the husband starts initiating for sex! Not all, but for some, they at least don't care to see if the partner is ready for it. Yet the women give in. It is just the story of the routine of a working woman's life, which is rather a monotonous one. As the cliché dialogue goes, "the show must go on".

CHAPTER EIGHT

THE MOTHER COURAGE

Nikhila grew up in a middle-class family and her mother was a single parent, who was meeting up with the daily expenses by being a tailor. Though their financial background was not so good, Nikhila's mother always did her best to provide whatever she needed. Nikhila was very happy and when she reached the age of marriage, her mother sent her off in marriage to a wealthy family.

Just like every girl of a marriageable age, Nikhila had lots of expectations and aspirations. The day of her marriage, everything was good, but the very next day her mother-in-law gave her one kilogram of fish and asked her to clean it. Nikhila was so shocked at the change in her mother-in-law's behaviour. Nikhila's mother had told her mother-in-law that Nikhila doesn't know much of kitchen chores and even after that her mother-in-law made her clean the entire fish by herself. She felt like crying when she was struggling to clean the fish, but somehow, she managed not to show her emotions to others.

That entire day, her mother-in-law made her work like a donkey. By evening, her mother-in-law asked her to have a bath at the pond near by the house. Though Nikhila was brought up in a middle-class family, she never had to take bath in a public place. There, everything was different. She somehow managed to hide her body and finished off her bath in few minutes and rushed to her room.

The very next day, she had her menstruation and things only got hard on her. She had to follow all the rules and regulations of that orthodox family. She was not allowed to enter the house from front door, but through the kitchen door, backside of the house. She started feeling like being treated like an untouchable. At night, she was not allowed to sleep on the bed those days of her periods; she had to instead sleep on the ground, on a carpet. She was not allowed to use sanitary pads; she had to use cloth alone. She felt it horrible having to wash those soaked clothes, soaked in blood, and reuse them. Whenever her mother called her, her mother-in-law always lingered around, and Nikhila never got a chance to share it with her mother.

What made her more pitiful was that Nikhila was allowed to visit her mother only once in three months. They never invited Nikhila's mother to the house or if at all she came, they never entertained her to stay there. Since travelling alone at night was unsafe, Nikhila's mother asked Nikhila to do as they instructed.

When she became pregnant, she thought she will get some relief, but her in laws were not that happy about her pregnancy. Her husband's sisters were the ones who were more indifferent to her as their brother didn't provide them as before, and they never paid a visit to her since her pregnancy.

Throughout pregnancy, she had to do daily chores and at time she got so discouraged that she wept whole night. Seventh month, she was taken to her own house and only after that, she got enough rest. Without many complications, she delivered her first baby, a baby girl whom she named Amyra. When her baby turned six months, she was taken back to her husband's house and her struggle started once and for all.

Most of her relatives and neighbours who came to see her pitied her as it is a baby girl. Their scornful comments made that clearer:

"Oh! It's a baby girl. It's okay, next time you will get a baby boy."

"I will pray that next time you will get a baby boy."

"It would have been great if you bore a boy child."

"Ah! One day she will have to go away, nah." etc...

Some even gave her advice about the pujas and rituals to get a baby boy. But Nikhila was very happy that she got a baby girl, a baby girl whom she can dress up, a baby girl who will inherit all her sarees and ornaments.

One day, there was a photoshoot in the family, and her husband mocked her in front of the entire family saying that she looked like an elephant holding a coconut. She felt so bad, but she suppressed her pain and brought a fake smile to defend her from the loud laughter that followed that comment.

In a year, she got pregnant again, but the child's growth was not normal; the child's head was bigger than the normal measures, and it was an abnormal child, hence she had to abort the baby. It was a baby boy adding to her grief.

The next time she delivered a child; it was a girl again. Nikhila was a fighter; she faced all the comments once again, but with a smile that showed her maturity. She promised to herself that she would be a wonderful mother to her two kids.

As children grew, so did the expenses. Her children were so talented that they practiced both dance and music. Such extra expenses put her again in the dim light of scrutiny, but she faced it all boldly and still strives to manage meeting all such expenses to make the future of her children brighter...

CHAPTER NINE

BEING UPRIGHT

Marriage is not just a divine covenant; one mistake done, and the lives of two people are at stake; the relationships of two families are put to stake. Often these days, people are in a hurry when it comes to marriage. Nowadays, many are settled abroad, and they have only few days leave to get the entire functions done.

Earlier marriages were done with proper enquiry about both the families, the groom, and the bride. Another factor is that nowadays many youngsters despise marriage; many ends up in live-in relationships. The parents are worried about their children ending up in any of these situations and they are anxious to somehow get them married to save their status in the society.

This is the story of two women, Nita and Praveena, who were friends from childhood days. Both were birds with the same feathers. They had similar aspirations about their future and life. Nita did TTC and became a lower primary school teacher, but Praveena was married off during her graduation and she was unable to pursue her studies.

Praveena was from a poor financial background and when this proposal came from a guy who was working in Dubai, her parents were in a hurry to send off her in marriage. The groom was very handsome, and they thought it was her luck that she got such a proposal from such a handsome man though she was dusky in complexion. Praveena herself was lured at the beauty of the groom and she wholeheartedly accepted the proposal.

Soon after Praveena's marriage with Jual, the family arranged the marriage of Jual's sister, Jewel. Jewel got a proposal from a wealthy family and her parents wanted that marriage to happen. The groom's family had demanded a huge dowry which was beyond the capability of the parents. They therefore asked Praveena if she could hand over her ornaments to be pawned to raise the huge sum, and Praveena gave her ornaments without any issue. But those ornaments turned out to be rolled gold and this led to a huge dispute within the family.

As the family could not raise the huge amount demanded from the groom's side the proposal was rejected. This raised the grudge of the family towards Praveena. She touched the feet of Jual and cried a lot as she didn't know anything about the rolled gold; she could not even think that her parents would do that to her. Jual forgave her, but his family remained cold to her. They started ill-treating her to the extent that they asked Praveena to cook separately for herself and Jual. Even during her both pregnancies they were unkind. They did not even help her in managing the kids that she had to keep them shut in the room while cooking. No one even bothered to check on the kids.

Jual asked for his share and with much struggle he managed to get it and they stayed separate from the family. Praveena saved every single penny that she could save, and she did a little bit of tailoring and embroidery to fend for her family. Praveena was the one who really struggled to save her family. Her husband handed over all his earnings to her and it was she who managed the expenses of the family with the little income they got. She was wise and she always saved some money by bargaining to the vendors. In five years, they managed to buy a small house for themselves.

When they finally started living a decent life, her in-laws came to visit them. The in laws thought Praveena would ward them off remembering all the torments they did to her, but to their shock, Praveena treated them well. Her in-laws saw for themselves how Praveena handled all the adverse situations and appreciated her perseverance.

It was at this time that Nita had called Praveena to invite Praveena to her wedding. Nita was getting married to a police officer and she was so proud to talk about the groom. Praveena went for the marriage, and it was a very grand wedding.

During initial days, everything sounded perfect for Nita, but in three months, things were not the same. From the time Nita's husband got a transfer, his mother and sisters started demanding money from her husband. Even though he was a police officer, he could not realize the intrigue and he was doing everything as they demanded. He had a soft corner for his family, and they were taking advantage of him. Nita was the one who had to face it all, living in the same family. They made life so horrible for Nita that they made her prepare all the food, and once the food was cooked, when Nita comes to have food almost all the side dishes would be over, especially the non-vegetarian items. They never left even a single piece of non-vegetarian dishes for her.

Luckily, in six months, she got a government job, and she decided to move near her workplace. When she decided to move, she asked his family for the jewels that were in his mother's custody. To her shock, all her jewels were sold off without her knowledge or consent. This incident made her husband realize the cunningness of his family members. Her husband felt so bad about all this and was so sorry for the wrongdoings of his family. He felt bad that he never paid attention to her words and trusted his family blindly. He told Nita that she could file a case against his mother if she wanted. Nita instead told that she doesn't want to take any such grave actions, but she wanted the price of her jewels just because it was the sweat and blood of her parents that got sold off even without her knowledge. She didn't want to make it public but since they are moving out to her new workplace, she wanted the amount worth her jewels to buy a new house at her workplace. Finally, his mother succumbed and gave her husband his share and the amount worth her jewels. Her decision to move out was the best decision ever.

After a few months, Nita met Praveena at a wedding party, and after the party, they went to the nearby park and had an open talk. They decided to stay in touch and fix each other's crowns just like queens for the rest of their lives...

CHAPTER TEN

RESILIENCE TO RENAISSANCE

Guidance is an important factor for the proper development of a person. Whatever the situation is, if one gets proper guidance, the person will be able to face it in a better way. This story will demonstrate what ignorance can do to you.

Nimmy grew up in a very remote village on the outskirts of Trivandrum. All she had in her life was her maternal grandparents. Her mother worked as a clerk in the town and used to come home only once in two weeks. Though she was sad about her mother's workaholic nature, her grandparents took care of her so well that she was not deeply affected by her mother's absence. Her father and mother were separated, and she had only a little knowledge about her father.

Nimmy was taken care of so well that she never even thought she had a father. When Nimmy joined school, the question was raised about who her father was, and she asked the same to her mother. Her mother told her to tell them that he is a doctor in Trivandrum itself. Nimmy never felt the need to ask further.

But when she reached Class V, she got a new classmate, Roopa. Roopa was the daughter of one of the acquaintances of Nimmy's mother. Roopa was quarrelsome, and often she used to fight with Nimmy for no reason. One such day, Roopa mocked Nimmy by telling her that Nimmy knows nothing about her father. This instance put Nimmy in doubt, and she started asking her mother about her father.

It was on a Sunday morning when no one else was at home that Nimmy's mother revealed her story. Nimmy's mother told her that her father was a mental patient, and the truth was hidden to her at the time of her marriage. Nimmy was having her tea, and at that very moment she felt that the entire world slipped away beneath her feet. She wanted to cry out loud. Yes, she was crying deep beneath her heart, but she didn't utter a noise outside. She felt giddy that she did not hear half of the story. She was suppressing her pain, keeping it all to herself, shut in her mind.

From the time Nimmy learnt about her father, she grew so short-tempered. She felt as if the whole world intrigued her and her mother into this plight. She grew aggressive toward everyone in the family. She started developing anger issues—sometimes she broke things in anger, sometimes she retorted others with bad words, and sometimes she grew so violent that she physically hurt others. She just didn't know how to manage all the anger that was building up a volcano within her.

By the time she reached class X, the thought that the genes of the family could pass on to her children started eating up her mind. Her father was sick; her paternal grandmother and her great-grandmother were sick. She did not know what to do, so all she could do was pray.

During the Catechism classes, she learnt that if she prays earnestly for anything after the Holy Communion, the prayers will surely be answered. She had deep faith and every time she prayed after the Holy Communion, she touched her tummy with one hand and her heart with the other hand and prayed for her womb. Any time she got an article based on mental health, she read it. For the years to come, she continued praying for her womb. To the people she trusted, she shared her cares and worries.

Years passed like that, and soon after her degree, she joined a Central University for her postgraduate studies. That was the first time she stayed away from her family. Life at the Central University was totally different from the life she had before.

The central university that she joined was in the Eastern part of India. It was all greenery around the campus that was spread across acres of land. There were buses and autos for transportation. The first semester, the campus was near her hostel, and it was just a walkable distance. That semester she got 96 percent. Unfortunately, by the second semester her department was changed to the other end of the university, at the newly constructed campus. It was newly built, and hence there was no greenery, and it was scorching hot. Lunch break was only fifteen minutes, and to go have lunch and come back for classes in fifteen minutes was a herculean task. The canteen served food that was too hot to eat hurriedly. In a hurry, she just had a papad and pickle for lunch. Days were going on like that. In the hostel room, there were three of them. She grew close to the one sleeping at the nearby bed who was a Physical Education student named Ansiya.

Every evening, she used to walk to the hostel mess with Ansiya. After the dinner, Ansiya's friends, including boys, used to gather before their hostel and used to have chitchats. Nimmy used to address everyone as brother; if it were North Indian guys, she used to call them 'bhaiyya'. Even though the guys used to taunt for calling them brothers as they are of the same age, she still only addressed them as brothers.

Life at the Central University was totally different. The worst part was that there were no wardens at the hostel, and so evenings were very convenient for lovers. They needed to enter the hostel only at 10 o'clock, and there was no attendance system to check on them. Nimmy always reached her room by 8 o'clock after dinner. She used to watch her favourite serials rather than having loose talks with the guys outside the hostel.

One such day, as she was browsing social media, she was added to a group named 'Contraband'. It was a group where they discussed and debated social issues. One such day there was a discussion about the Catholic Church. As the discussion heated up, Nimmy joined, as there were only a few people who were talking for the church. As she put on her comments, there was another guy named Manu Mathew who was putting his comments as well. In the heat of the discussion, to her surprise, both were making the same comments in support of the church. Thus, they became friends; they exchanged their numbers, and she saved his number as "cool guy." As their friendship thickened, she shared her cares and worries, and soon he became her only solace. She could call him at any point of the night to share any problem. That was Nimmy's first deep friendship with a boy, and she started falling in love with him. She never shared such feelings to him but deep within her mind, she was falling in love with his genuine self. In a month she was developing head on heels love for him. She even shared it with her family and friends, but not to him.

It was at that time that her family planned to celebrate the 70th wedding anniversary of her grandparents. It was a grand celebration that they had planned. They had Shivaratri holidays in the beginning of March, so she went home one week before the planned date of her arrival.

When she reached home, all were so surprised that she came. They were all getting ready for shopping, and Nimmy decided to stay home to take care of her grandmother, who had Alzheimer's. She had reached home at 8'o'clock, and she had been taking care of her grandmother ever since. She hadn't even brushed her teeth, so by 2 p.m. she decided to get freshened up. But by the time she was out, her grandmother had fallen, and one of her hands was dislocated. Her family came back soon but her maternal uncle kiddingly said that it was all because of Nimmy's carelessness. Though she said it as a joke, this affected her so much.

Nimmy was so deeply affected by her uncle's comment that she used to cry when no one was around. She was afraid hearing the painful cries of her grandmother. She was so much in fear that she thought her grandmother would die. She had sleepless nights taking care of her grandmother. While the family was feasting with non-vegetarian food, she prayed for the speedy recovery of her grandmother. At night, every cry of her grandmother woke her up in fear while others had a sound sleep. Meanwhile, she used to call Manu and her other friends and weep about all that was happening. She was so exhausted, but still, she cleaned all the vomit of her grandmother by herself. She was the one who used to take her grandmother to the hospital. By the time she returned to the campus, she was totally exhausted.

Nimmy was so dear to everyone at the campus that her classmate boys came to pick her up from the gate to the hostel early morning. She freshened up and went to attend the class that day itself, though she was exhausted. Much to her shock, she learnt that the second semester exams were going to start soon. She got worried as she hadn't gone through any of her notes in the past few months. She started waking up the whole night to study. Three nights she didn't sleep at all. Meanwhile, during some conversations with Manu, she expressed her feelings for him, and adding to her shock, he declined and said he can see her only as a friend. This shook her off, and she went out of her mind gradually. She was not sleeping; she was not eating; she was not attending classes regularly. Her friends noticed these changes, and all of them together brought her to a room to discuss it all. Nimmy started sharing, but nothing of her sharing sounded sane. They tried their best, but she was not eating anything. They called her, and along with other guy friends, they asked her to delete her Facebook account.

That night Nimmy sat before her laptop to delete her Facebook account. Suddenly a message popped in, and the person who messaged her seems to know everything about her. She was quite ignorant to handle social media, or is it that her mind's overthinking that she thought it was Manu who was messaging her? To her surprise and shock, the person started telling her many things that she thought only she knew, and the person made her type out everything she was feeling and started to control her thoughts. The whole night the chat continued, and Nimmy, who thought it was Manu, was made to feel that he was coming to see her that morning. But sadly, when she was called out of the hostel, when she rushed to see the love of her life, it was her family who had come. She got agitated and started calling out Manu's name. Her family forcefully took her to a nearby mental hospital, where she was sedated and taken to Kerala. Her last memory was being asked by her friends to sleep.

When she woke up, it was an unpleasant feeling. She felt being pushed and pulled. The next time she was in sense, she was in a cell, and the man lying in the adjacent cell was showing his penis to her. She overheard nurses commenting about her that she had slapped one of the nurses, and so she was put in the cell. When she woke up next morning, she found the maid cleaning the entire area. The doctor came by the cell, looked at her, instructed something to the team, and he left. Thereafter she was taken to the common area where all the patients were seated, ladies on one side and the gents on the other. Some men were going on showing pervert actions, and she was quite drowsy to perceive them.

Nimmy was quite arrogant, and she was put in a cell full of urine. Without cleaning the room, they had put it here as a punishment. She wanted to urinate, but they didn't open her from the cell, and she had to urinate in that cell. Nurses asked her to leave the bathroom door open while she had a bath. She felt totally trapped. The entire time she called out Manu's name. Whoever passed by her cell, she inquired about Manu. If she heard a funeral procession, she cried and asked everyone if it was her Manu. She was not at all in her senses, but she knew his phone number by heart. She started asking everyone to call him and to ask him to help her out from there.

Two months passed, and she got discharged. She tried to call her friends, but her mother destroyed the mobile phone. Thus, she was completely shut off from anything and everything. As she was recovering, she recollected all the dialogues she overheard at the hospital. To her mind came the term bipolar disorder. That was what she only remembered from the dialogues of the nurses.

When she recovered, she joined a college that was in her village. She got a new phone under the condition that she would not contact anyone from the past. A year passed. She had her new Facebook account, and she searched for her old friends. Manu's phone number was switched off; maybe he blocked her or changed the sim. Some friends responded well, while others didn't respond.

Of all the replies she got, one message shook her mind. It was another friend of hers whose name was also Manu. He said being her friend was his worst situation, and now he is afraid to befriend any girl. She was quite perplexed and wondered why he was talking like that because, by no way, this guy would know what happened to her. By enquiring further, she realized what happened. Her friends had called this Manu and said that she was undergoing all of what happened because of him. Then only she realized that she had saved real Manu's name as "cool guy." Her friends searched the name Manu, and they got this Manu's contact. Everything was upside down, completely messed up. Thus, she lost a friend because of all this scenario. He was not ready to hear her explanation, so he blocked her. She felt so lost, but she regained all the pieces and started afresh.

Today she is a postgraduate in MBA. As she became technologically advanced, she understood what happened that night at the central university. Someone had used the technology of "Any desk" to fool her. It was the dawn of April Fool that she was made to convince that Manu would come, and she shouted "Manu," "Manu," seeing her family, and she was taken to the mental hospital.

Nimmy studied more about her condition. She understood that bipolar disorder is actually a boon. She was not in the category of the ones with suicidal tendencies. She learnt that the most intelligent infants are the ones who tend to be bipolar, and it is indeed a boon. It is just that she can't handle strong emotions, and her mental strength to face situations is weak, and that is the only thing she needs to take care of. She taught herself to be bold, and thus she accepted her medical condition.

The next time she visited her hospital and the doctor told her that this mental state happens as episodes that would reoccur. If she had her medications properly, it would not affect her mind. The moment she started trusting her doctor and seriously took care of having the medications properly, she started doing really well, and today she is the General Manager of a company who has every chance to be the next CEO of the company. That's why they say when life gives you a lemon, make a lemonade out of it...

CHAPTER ELEVEN

SHADOWS OF ENLIGHTENMENT

Sister Maria gripped the worn leather strap of her suitcase, her fingers trembling slightly as she gazed up at the towering stone walls of the convent. A sense of both excitement and trepidation swirled within her. This was the moment she had been preparing for her entire life – the start of a new chapter dedicated to serving God and her community.

"Welcome, my child," a gentle voice called out, and Maria turned to see an older nun approaching her, a warm smile on her face. "I am Sister Agnes. It is a pleasure to have you join our community."

"Thank you, Sister," Maria replied, her voice soft yet full of conviction. "I am honoured to be here. I hope to serve the Lord and this convent to the best of my abilities."

Sister Agnes placed a hand on Maria's arm, the gesture both maternal and reassuring. "We are delighted to have you. Come, let me show you to your quarters. I'm sure you must be weary from your journey."

As Maria followed Sister Agnes through the serene hallways, she couldn't help but marvel at the beauty that surrounded her. Sunlight streamed in through the large windows, casting a warm glow over the polished floors and intricate tapestries that adorned the walls. The rhythmic chanting of the nuns echoed through the corridors, a soothing soundtrack to her new home.

"Here we are," Sister Agnes announced, stopping in front of a modest wooden door. "This will be your room. I trust you'll find it comfortable."

Maria pushed open the door, revealing a cozy space with a simple bed, a small desk, and a wardrobe. It was a far cry from the luxuries she had grown up with, but she couldn't help but feel a sense of peace wash over her. This was her new sanctuary, a place where she could dedicate herself entirely to a life of service.

"Thank you, Sister," Maria said, turning to face Agnes with a grateful smile. "It's perfect."

"Excellent." Agnes clasped her hands together, her expression brightening. "Now, let me introduce you to the rest of our community. I'm sure they're eager to meet you."

As Maria followed the older nun through the winding corridors, she couldn't help but feel a sense of anticipation. This was the moment she had been waiting for – the start of her new life as a sister in the convent. She knew the road ahead would not be an easy one, but her determination to live a life of faith and service burned brighter than ever before.

"Sisters, I'd like to introduce you to our newest member, Sister Maria," Agnes announced, placing a hand on Maria's shoulder. "She has come to us all the way from the city, eager to join our community and dedicate herself to the Lord's work."

A chorus of warm greetings and welcoming smiles met Maria's gaze, and she felt a surge of excitement and belonging. These were her new sisters, her family in this sacred place.

"It's a pleasure to meet you all," Maria said, her voice clear and steady. "I look forward to working alongside you in service to our faith and our community."

Later that evening, as Maria lay in her bed, staring up at the vaulted ceiling, she couldn't help but reflect on the journey that had brought her here. The path had not been an easy one, marked by moments of doubt and uncertainty, but her faith had always been her guiding light. Now, as she prepared to embark on this new chapter, she felt a renewed sense of purpose and determination.

"Lord, guide me," she whispered into the stillness of the night, her eyes closing as she offered a silent prayer. "Help me to be an instrument of your will, to inspire change and bring your message of love and compassion to all those I encounter."

The next day as Sister Maria settled into the daily routines of the convent, she noticed subtle cracks in the façade of piety and devotion that had initially captivated her. The serene tranquillity of the countryside was often disrupted by the whispers and petty squabbles among her fellow nuns, and she couldn't help but feel a growing sense of unease.

During a morning prayer session, Sister Maria observed Sister Agnes carefully arranging her habit, ensuring it fell just so, her eyes darting around the room as if seeking approval from the others. When it came time to pass the collection plate, Sister Agnes deftly slipped a few extra bills into the basket, her lips curling into a self-satisfied smile.

Later that day, as Sister Maria assisted in the convent's kitchen, she overheard Father Thomas engaged in a lively discussion with a few of the younger nuns, animatedly describing the latest technological gadgets he had acquired. He was the Rector of that parish. His eyes shone with excitement, a stark contrast to the solemn demeanour one might expect from a clergy.

Troubled by these observations, Sister Maria sought out Sister Lucy, a gentle soul who had been assigned to show her around the convent. "Sister Lucy," Maria began, her brow furrowed, "I can't help but notice some... discrepancies between the ideals we profess and the way we actually conduct ourselves here."

Sister Lucy's eyes widened, and she glanced around nervously before responding in a hushed tone. "I know, Sister Maria. It's something I've struggled with myself. The others can be... quite worldly at times." She paused, wringing her hands. "But you mustn't judge them too harshly. We all have our weaknesses, and the path to true devotion is not an easy one."

Maria nodded, her resolve hardening. "I understand, Sister Lucy. But I can't help feeling that if we are to truly serve the Lord, we must strive to live up to the standards we set for ourselves." She placed a gentle hand on Lucy's arm. "I believe we are called to be beacons of hope, not mere reflections of the world around us."

Lucy offered a small, uncertain smile. "I admire your conviction, Sister Maria. But changing the ways of this place will not be easy. The others can be... resistant to change."

"Then I shall have to be persistent," Maria declared, her eyes shining with determination. "For if we cannot lead by example, how can we expect to inspire others?"

In the days that followed, Sister Maria's observations only deepened her concern. During a charity event organized by the convent, she watched in dismay as the nuns primped and preened, more focused on the appearance of their habits and the arrangement of the refreshments than on the actual needs of the people they were meant to serve. As she gazed out at the gathering, she couldn't help but wonder if the true purpose of their mission had been obscured by the trappings of power and status.

That evening, as Maria knelt in prayer, she felt a sense of conflict welling within her. The convent she had envisioned, a place of pure devotion and selfless service, seemed to be at odds with the reality she was now witnessing. She prayed for guidance, for the strength to navigate these murky waters, and for the courage to speak the truth, even if it meant challenging the very foundations of the institution she had come to serve.

Sister Maria sat in the small chapel, the flickering candlelight casting a warm glow on the intricate stained-glass windows. She had spent the better part of the morning in quiet reflection, her mind grappling with the unsettling realizations that had unfolded since her arrival at the convent.

"Lord, guide me," she whispered, her voice barely audible. "I came here seeking to serve You, to live a life of devotion and purpose. But now, I find myself questioning the very foundations of this community."

The sound of soft footsteps interrupted her prayer, and Maria turned to see the gentle face of Sister Lucy approaching.

"Sister Maria," Lucy said, her voice laced with concern. "I noticed you had not joined the others for morning prayers. Is everything all right?"

Maria offered a weary smile. "I'm afraid I have been struggling, Sister Lucy. The things I've witnessed here have left me... unsettled."

Lucy nodded, her eyes reflecting a similar conflict. "I understand. The ways of this convent can be... complicated. There is a tension between the ideals we profess and the realities we face."

Maria's gaze met Lucy's, a silent understanding passing between them. "I feel so torn, Sister. I came here with such conviction, but now I find myself questioning everything. How can we truly serve the Lord when there is so much self-interest and hypocrisy all around us?"

Lucy placed a gentle hand on Maria's shoulder. "It is a burden we all carry, to some degree. The world beyond these walls can seep in, testing our faith and our resolve. But we must not lose sight of the reason we are here."

Maria nodded, her fingers tightening around the wooden rail. "I know, but it is so difficult. I see Sister Agnes and Father Thomas, and their actions seem so at odds with the very principles we are meant to uphold. How can I remain true to my calling when I'm surrounded by such... contradictions?"

"It is a constant struggle," Lucy admitted, her voice soft. "But we must not lose hope. Our faith is not defined by the failings of others, but by our own commitment to living according to God's will."

Maria's gaze lifted, her eyes shining with determination. "Then that is what I must focus on. I came here to serve, to make a difference. I cannot allow the actions of others to diminish my own purpose."

Lucy smiled, a glimmer of pride in her eyes. "That is the spirit, Sister Maria. We must be the change we wish to see in this place. With your guidance and unwavering faith, perhaps we can inspire others to walk a more righteous path."

Maria reached out and squeezed Lucy's hand, a newfound resolution settling within her. "Then that is what I shall do. I may not be able to change the hearts of everyone here, but I can strive to live by the principles I hold dear. And perhaps, in time, others will see the light and join me."

The two women stood, their shared determination fuming in the air. As they made their way back to the convent, Maria felt a renewed sense of purpose, her steps more assured. She would face the challenges ahead with steadfast faith, determined to be a beacon of hope in this place that had once filled her with such disillusionment.

The next day morning she dressed quickly, Maria made her way to the chapel. As she knelt before the altar, she poured out her heart in prayer. "Lord, grant me the wisdom and strength to do Your will. Help me to inspire change in this place, to reignite the true spirit of service and devotion."

Feeling a renewed sense of purpose, Maria set out to organize the community service project she had envisioned. Gathering a small group of like-minded sisters, including the ever-faithful Sister Lucy, they began to plan an outreach program to assist the local orphanage.

As word of the project spread, however, Maria soon encountered resistance from an unexpected source – Sister Agnes and Father Thomas. "A community service project?" Sister Agnes scorned; her manicured brow furrowed in disdain. "Surely we have more pressing matters to attend to, like the upcoming fundraiser. That is where we should be focusing our efforts."

Father Thomas, ever the diplomat, tried to interject. "Now, now, let's not dismiss this idea so quickly. Perhaps we could find a way to incorporate both the service project and the fundraiser. But Sister Agnes was having none of it, "The fundraiser is what brings in the donations that we need to maintain this convent. We can't afford to divert resources away from that."

Maria felt her heart sink. She had hoped the others would see the value in reaching out to those in need, but it was clear that their priorities lay elsewhere. Squaring her shoulders, she met Sister Agnes's steely gaze. Maria said, "The purpose of this convent is to serve God and His people, not to amass wealth and status. If we lose sight of that, then we have failed in our calling." The words hung in the air, thick with tension. Sister Agnes opened her mouth to retort, but Father Thomas raised a hand, silencing her.

"Sister Maria has a point. We must never forget the true reason for our vocation." He turned to Maria, his expression contemplative, "I will speak with the Mother Superior about allocating resources for your project. Let's see what we can do to make it a success." Maria felt a surge of hope, but Sister Agnes's expressions told a different story. "This is a mistake," she muttered, before storming out of the room. As the others dispersed, Maria found herself alone with Sister Lucy. The young nun placed a gentle hand on her arm and said, "You stood your ground, Maria. I'm proud of you."

Maria sighed, some of the tension leaving her shoulders. "I only hope I can inspire the others to do the same. This convent needs to remember its purpose." Sister Lucy nodded solemnly, "With your guidance, perhaps we can rekindle the true spirit of this place. But it will not be easy."

"I know," Maria replied, her gaze resolute and continued, "But I'm prepared to face whatever challenges lay ahead. This is my calling, and I will not falter." The two women shared a moment of quiet understanding before heading off to their respective duties, each carrying the weight of their convictions.

In the days that followed, Sister Maria poured her heart and soul into the community service project. She rallied the sisters who shared her vision, organizing supply drives, volunteering at the orphanage, and leading by example. The work was often gruelling, but Maria found solace in the joy and gratitude of the children they served. However, the resistance from Sister Agnes and Father Thomas only grew more pronounced. During a meeting with the Mother Superior, they voiced their concerns about the project's impact on the convent's resources and reputation.

"This outreach program is taking valuable time and money away from our other priorities," Sister Agnes argued, "We simply cannot afford such distractions." Father Thomas, ever the diplomat, tried to mediate. "Perhaps we could find a way to balance the needs of the community with our own obligations. Surely there is a middle ground we can reach."

But Maria refused to back down. "Our vows call us to serve others, not to hoard our resources for ourselves. These children need us, and we have a moral obligation to help them." The Mother Superior listened intently; her brow furrowed in thought. After a long pause, she spoke, "Sister Maria, I admire your passion and commitment. However, we must also consider the practical realities of running this convent."

Maria's heart sank, but she refused to give up. "Mother Superior, if I may – this project is not just about the children. It is about reigniting the true spirit of this place, about reminding us of all of our sacred calling. Surely that is worth the investment of time and resources?"

The Mother Superior's gaze softened, and Maria could see the conflict in her eyes, "I will consider your proposal, Sister Maria. But I cannot promise any immediate changes." As Maria left the meeting, she felt a mixture of disappointment and determination. She knew the road ahead would be long and arduous, but she was more resolved than ever to inspire the change she believed in.

In the days following the heated exchange with Sister Agnes and Father Thomas, a growing sense of unease had settled within Maria. She could not shake the nagging suspicion that something was amiss in the convent's financial dealings. Determined to uncover the truth, she had discreetly pored over the books, her fingers trembling as the evidence began to mount.

Now, as she faced the council, Maria knew there was no turning back. "Sisters," she began, her voice steady despite the weight of the words she was about to utter, "I have discovered that a significant portion of the funds kept for our charitable outreach have been misappropriated." Gasps echoed through the room, and Sister

Agnes's eyes widened in alarm. Father Thomas shifted uncomfortably in his seat, avoiding Maria's gaze.

The Mother Superior raised a hand, silencing the murmurs. "This is a grave accusation, Sister Maria. Do you have proof of these allegations?" Maria nodded, her expression resolute, "I have meticulously reviewed the financial records, and the discrepancies are undeniable. Funds that were meant to aid the less fortunate have been diverted for personal gain."

Sister Agnes rose from her chair, her face flushed with indignation. "This is an outrage! Sister Maria is clearly making unfounded claims to undermine our work and our standing in the community." Father Thomas cleared his throat, his brow furrowed in contemplation. "Perhaps we should hear Sister Maria out before rushing to judgment. If there is indeed a breach of trust, it must be addressed."

The Mother Superior raised a hand, silencing the growing tension, "Sister Maria, I understand the gravity of your findings. However, the implications of such an accusation are far-reaching. We must proceed with the utmost care and discretion."

Maria took a deep breath, her gaze unwavering. "I understand the sensitivity of this matter, Mother Superior. But I cannot in good conscience remain silent. Our mission is to serve the Lord and care for those in need. If we have betrayed that trust, it is our duty to confront it, no matter the personal cost."

The room fell silent, the weight of Maria's words hanging in the air. Sister Lucy, who had been sitting quietly in the corner, spoke up, her voice trembling with emotion. "Sister Maria is right. We must uphold the integrity of our faith and our calling, even if it means facing the consequences of our actions."

The Mother Superior studied the faces of the council, her own expression troubled. "This is a serious matter that requires our full attention. We shall convene a special meeting to thoroughly investigate these allegations and determine the appropriate course of action."

Maria nodded, her heart heavy with the gravity of the situation. As the council members began to file out of the room, she caught Sister Agnes's gaze, a silent challenge passing between them. Maria knew that the path ahead would be arduous, but she was prepared to face it head-on, her unwavering commitment to her faith and her principles guiding her every step.

In the quiet solitude of her cell, Maria knelt in prayer, her hands clasped tightly. "Lord, grant me the strength to navigate this ethical dilemma with wisdom and courage. May my actions be guided by Your will, and may they bring about the transformation this convent so desperately needs."

As the weight of the impending investigation settled upon her, Maria steeled her resolve. She knew that the road ahead would be fraught with challenges, but she was determined to see it through, no matter the personal cost. For in her heart, she believed that the truth, however painful, would ultimately set them free.

The morning after the tense convent meeting, Sister Maria awoke with a renewed sense of purpose. Despite the turmoil that had gripped the community, she felt a glimmer of hope stirring within her. As she made her way to the chapel for her daily prayers, she couldn't help but notice a subtle shift in the air – a newfound contemplation among her fellow sisters.

As Maria knelt before the altar, she offered a heartfelt prayer for guidance. "Lord, grant me the strength to continue on this path, to be a beacon of hope in the face of adversity. Help me inspire change, not through force, but through the power of your unwavering love." When the prayer concluded, Maria rose and made her way to the courtyard, where she found Sister Lucy tending to the small garden. The younger nun greeted her with a warm smile, her eyes reflecting a newfound resolve.

"Sister Maria," Lucy began, "I've been thinking a lot about our conversation the other day. About the importance of staying true to our calling, even when the path ahead seems uncertain." Maria nodded, placing a gentle hand on Lucy's shoulder. "It is not an easy road, my dear, but one that is worth walking. The Lord has placed us here for a reason, and we must have faith that He will guide us."

"I know," Lucy replied, her voice soft but steady, "And I want you to know that I'm with you, Sister. Whatever challenges may come, I will stand by your side." Maria felt a surge of gratitude, her heart swelling with the knowledge that she had an ally in this battle for the convent's soul, "Thank you, Sister Lucy. Your support means more to me than you know."

As the two women continued their conversation, they were joined by an unexpected visitor – Father Thomas. The priest's usually confident demeanour seemed tempered by a touch of humility.

"Sisters," he said, inclining his head respectfully. "I must apologize for my earlier reluctance to fully embrace the importance of your community service project. I've had time to reflect, and I realize now that the true measure of our faith lies not in the four walls of our institution, but in the service we provide to those in need."

The three stood in contemplative silence for a moment, the weight of Father Thomas's words settling over them. Then, Lucy spoke up, her voice brimming with hope, "If Father Thomas is willing to stand with us, then perhaps others will follow. Maybe this scandal can be the catalyst for real change within the convent."

As the day wore on, Maria noticed subtle shifts in the behaviour of her fellow nuns. Some approached her with tentative questions, their eyes reflecting a newfound humility. Others sought her counsel, eager to understand how they could better align their actions with the convent's spiritual mission. One such encounter occurred during the afternoon's communal prayer session. As Maria knelt, lost in contemplation, Sister Agnes approached and placed a gentle hand on her shoulder.

"Sister Maria," Agnes began, her voice uncharacteristically soft. "I... I must apologize for my behaviour. I've been so focused on appearances and status that I've lost sight of what truly matters. Your example has made me realize how far I've strayed from our calling."

Maria felt a surge of hope at Agnes's words. "I would be honoured to have your help, Sister. Together, we can show the world the true spirit of this convent."

As the days passed, Maria witnessed a gradual transformation within the community. The nuns, once consumed by petty rivalries and self-interest, began to rediscover the joy of selfless service. Fundraisers and charity events took on a new purpose, with the focus shifting from materialism to genuine outreach.

Even the Mother Superior, who had initially expressed reservations about Maria's bold actions, began to see the merit in her approach. During a private meeting, the older nun placed a weathered hand on Maria's arm, her eyes shining with a newfound respect, "Sister Maria, I must commend you for your unwavering commitment to our faith and our community. It is not easy to challenge the financial needs to keep up the status of the convent, but your example has inspired us all to reflect on our priorities. I believe, with your leadership, we can reclaim the true spirit of this convent."

Maria felt a surge of humility and gratitude. "Mother Superior, I am merely a vessel for the Lord's work. It is His will that has guided me, and it is His love that has transformed the hearts of our sisters."

With a contented sigh, Maria turned and made her way to the chapel, ready to offer a prayer of gratitude for the blessings that had been bestowed upon her and her community. She was no longer the idealistic newcomer, but a beacon of hope, inspiring change and guiding her fellow sisters towards a more authentic spiritual life.

CHAPTER TWELVE

SHATTERED ILLUSIONS

The soft glow of twinkling lights and the gentle humming of lively chatter filled the air as Raj navigated through the bustling party. His eyes scanned the crowd, searching for a familiar face, when suddenly, he found himself captivated by the sight of a stunningly beautiful woman across the room.

She stood there, radiant in a flowing sari, her dark eyes sparkling with an alluring confidence. Raj felt a jolt of electricity course through him, and in that moment, it was as if the world around them had faded into the background. Gathering his courage, he made his way towards her, his heart pounding with a mixture of excitement and nerves.

"Hi, I'm Raj," he introduced himself, his voice tinged with an endearing shyness.

The woman turned to face him, a coy smile playing on her lips. "I'm Priya. It's a pleasure to meet you."

Their initial exchange was tentative, but as the conversation progressed, Raj found himself drawn in by Priya's charm and captivating presence. She spoke with a flirtatious tone, her words weaving a spell that enveloped him. Raj, ever the romantic, was taken aback by her allure, his idealistic views on love and relationships fuelling his growing infatuation.

Raj and Priya lost themselves in each other's company, their laughter and playful talks filling the air. Time slipped by unnoticed, and it wasn't until Raj's friend, Anisha, gently interrupted them that he realized how long they had been engrossed in their own little world.

"Raj, I see you've met Priya," Anisha said, her warm smile hinting at a knowing look. "I'm glad you two are getting along so well."

Raj felt a flush of embarrassment, but Priya's hand on his arm quickly dispelled any awkwardness. "Yes, we were just getting to know each other," she replied, her voice dripping with charm.

Anisha's eyes sparkled with a hint of concern, but she simply nodded and excused herself, leaving Raj and Priya to continue their captivating conversation.

As the party ended, Raj found himself reluctant to part ways with Priya. The connection they had forged felt electric, and he knew he couldn't bear the thought of not seeing her again.

"I don't want this night to end," he confessed, his eyes filled with a mixture of hope and trepidation.

Priya's lips curled into a coy smile. "Then let's make sure it doesn't," she replied, her hand gently caressing his arm.

In that moment, Raj knew he had found something special. The whirlwind of emotions he felt was both exciting and overwhelming, but he was powerless to resist the allure of Priya's captivating presence.

Over the following weeks, Raj and Priya's relationship blossomed with a fuelling intensity. They spent every spare moment together, exploring the city's vibrant streets, sharing intimate conversations, and thrilled of their newfound love.

Raj's family, steeped in traditional values, initially expressed some reservations about the speed of the relationship, but Priya's charm and Raj's unwavering devotion soon won them over. Before long, Raj found himself on one knee, gazing into Priya's eyes as he poured out his heart, asking her to be his wife.

Priya's response was immediate and unequivocal. "Yes, Raj, I will marry you!" she exclaimed, her eyes shining with joy.

The engagement was celebrated with a grand ceremony, filled with the vibrant colours and rich traditions of Indian culture. Raj's heart swelled with pride and happiness as he watched Priya, radiant in her bridal finery, become his betrothed.

As the festivities unfolded, Raj couldn't help but feel a sense of overwhelming bliss. He had found the love of his life, and together, they would embark on a journey of eternal happiness. The future stretched out before them, brimming with the promise of a fairytale romance.

Little did Raj know that the cracks in their perfect facade were already beginning to form, threatening to shatter the ideal-like world he had so carefully constructed.

The air was thick with anticipation as Raj stood at the centre of the bustling wedding preparations, his heart racing with a mixture of excitement and nervousness. After the whirlwind romance that had swept him off his feet, the day he had been dreaming of had finally arrived – his marriage to his enchanting Priya.

Raj's family had initially expressed some reservations about the speed of their courtship, but their concerns had quickly melted away as they witnessed the genuine affection and compatibility between the young couple. Priya had won them over with her charming demeanour and her genuine interest in their traditions and values.

As Raj watched the vivid decorations being put in place and the vibrant fabrics being draped across the venue, he couldn't help but feel a sense of pride and accomplishment. This was the culmination of his dreams – to build a life with the woman he loved, surrounded by the warmth and support of his family.

Priya, radiant in her ornated bridal attire and jewellery, glided gracefully through the bustling preparations; her eyes sparkling with a mixture of joy and anticipation. Raj's breath caught in his throat every time he caught a glimpse of her, marvelling at how truly beautiful she was, both inside and out.

As the priest recited the traditional mantras, Raj listened intently, his mind focused on the words that would unite him with Priya forever. When it was time for them to exchange their vows, Raj held Priya's hands in his own, his eyes shining with sincerity with a promise to cherish her for the rest of his life and vow to be a faithful and devoted husband, to support her in all her endeavours, and to create a life filled with love, laughter, and endless possibilities.

As the ceremony reached its climax there was a chorus of cheers and blessings, showering the newlyweds with rose petals and traditional sweets. Raj and Priya exchanged a tender embrace, their hearts overflowing with the promise of a future filled with endless possibilities.

In the days that followed, they spent their evenings strolling through the vibrant streets of the city, hand in hand, marvelling at the way their lives had come together in such a whirlwind of love and devotion. Priya joined for PSC coaching and Raj wholeheartedly supported her.

However, beneath the surface of their fairytale romance, there were subtle cracks beginning to form. Raj couldn't help but notice his newly wed wife being so busy with her phone all the while, but he kept those concerns aside and looked at the brighter side. Little did he know that the foundations of their relationship were about to be tested in ways he could never have imagined.

That evening, as they prepared for dinner with Raj's family, Priya excused herself to freshen up. Raj used the opportunity to discreetly check her phone, his heart pounding. He knew it was a breach of trust, but the lingering doubts had become too much to ignore. Raj's fingers trembled as he scrolled through Priya's messages, his eyes widening as he stumbled upon a conversation with a number he didn't recognize. The messages were explicit, filled with flirtatious chats and suggestive emojis. Raj's felt his world crashing down around him as he read through the messages.

Just then, the bathroom door opened, and Priya emerged, her eyes widening in alarm as she caught Raj with her phone in his hands. "Raj! What are you doing?" she exclaimed, her voice laced with panic. Raj felt his heart racing, the betrayal affecting him so badly. "Priya, who is Ranjit?" he asked, his voice trembling with a mixture of hurt and anger.

Priya's expression shifted, her features hardening as she snatched the phone from his hands. "That's none of your business," she snapped, her usual charm replaced by a defensive aggression.

In Raj's mind the pieces of the puzzle were slowly coming together. "Is he... is he your lover?" he asked, his voice barely above a whisper.

Priya's silence was all the confirmation he needed. Raj felt his world crumbling, the idealized vision of their perfect marriage shattering before his eyes. He had trusted Priya completely, and now he felt like a fool for doing so.

Anisha's words from their earlier conversation echoed in his mind. "Raj, you need to be honest with yourself. Don't ignore the signs, even if they're uncomfortable to face."

Raj took a deep breath, steeling himself for the confrontation he knew was coming. "Priya, we need to talk."

Priya instantly apologized and assured him that she would mend her ways. Raj was hopeful but the next morning when he woke up, he felt an urge to check her phone and found that she had sent her nude photos to Ranjit. This was beyond his tolerance.

That afternoon Raj met Anisha and shared it all. Anisha told Raj that when she enquired about Priya, she learnt some unpleasant news that most of the days that Priya went out in the name of PSC coaching she didn't attend those classes and was wandering with a guy. Raj asked if it was Ranjit, showing his picture from social media. Shockingly it was some other guy. This made both of them question about Priya's character.

Anisha brought up an idea and she gave him a new SIM and asked Raj to message Priya as though he is a stranger and that by mistake, he messaged her, mistaking her to be someone else. Raj liked the idea, and he did so. Anisha asked him to let her know when Priya replies.

That evening Raj got the reply from Priya asking who he was. Raj typed that he is a pet shop owner and asked if she wanted a Persian cat. She declined and from then there was no other messages from Priya's side. This gave some hope to Raj but the next morning he received a good morning message from Priya. He continued the chat and led the chat to a flirtatious way, and he was shocked to see that she sent her selfie showing off the cleavage and as the chat continued by the evening, she sent him her nude photos. That was quite unexpected and broke Raj completely.

Anisha was shocked as well to learn that Priya could sent her nude photos even to a stranger. Anisha enquired more about Priya and learnt that she had open relationships with many guys before and after the marriage.

It was at that time Priya told him that she was pregnant. Raj was in dilemma about whether it was his own child or one out of the wedlock. He decided to leave her and left her after a heated argument.

After few weeks he started getting her nude pics and sex videos from unknown numbers, and even from his own friends. Priya had turned a prostitute and in a video, he saw her pregnant belly. He could not believe that she was sleeping with other guys even in pregnancy. He thought she must have aborted the child, but she was having physical relationship with other guys even while she was at the advance stage of pregnancy.

Raj changed his SIM and started living his life in his way. But after some months, he got a message in his old WhatsApp from Priya letting him know that she has delivered a baby boy with a picture of the child. Raj was again in dilemma but the thought that what if the child is his, he visited her at the hospital and did his duties as a husband.

At this point of time, Raj was quite depressed about his life. He didn't know what to do, and how to face the life ahead of him. As the baby grew, he had all the features of Raj and he needed no DNA test to be sure that it was his baby. The baby looked just like him. He decided to live for his child. Seeing the motherly affection that Priya showed to the baby gave him one final hope that at least she would change from then.

Everything was fine till the baby reached six months. After that there was some changes in Priya. She seemed to be engaged on her phone more than attending the baby. It was Raj who took care of the baby mostly. She was chatting with other guys even at night. Raj tried to make her understand but she seemed disinterested to mend her ways. In a month, she started going back to her old ways, her whore life. She even went for an audition of erotic movies, moving to another level of immoral life.

Raj was at the verge of depression, but Anisha's friendship and the support of his family helped him to face the situation the way he should face. He started living with his parents, who took care of the baby, and he started a business. His business became his driving force in fighting back the adversities of his personal life. As months passed, his business became a success and he just had one goal in his life- to bring up his son as a responsible citizen, guided by moral values and principles.

CHAPTER THIRTEEN

RECLAIMING LIFE

Rajesh wiped the sweat from his brow as he stepped out into the scorching Middle Eastern sun. The air was thick with the scent of diesel and the piercing noise of the construction machinery. This was his life now - a far cry from the quiet, pastoral town he had left behind in India.

From his 30 years age, Rajesh had left the comforts of home for the job of a weary migrant worker. The decision had not been an easy one, but the promise of a better life for his family had compelled him to make the journey. He worked 20 years of his lifetime in the Middle East fending for his family. He hardly took leaves or vacations. Now, as he made his way to the construction site, he couldn't help but wonder if he had made the right choice.

Rajesh shared a cramped room with five other men, all of them hailing from different parts of India. The accommodations were uncomfortable, with little more than a thin mattress and a small wardrobe to call their own. The food they lived on was equally meagre - a daily diet of rice, lentils, and the occasional vegetable, all prepared in a communal kitchen.

Despite the challenging conditions, Rajesh maintained a steadfast determination. Each month, he dutifully sent a portion of his earnings back to his family in India - a wife and two children he had not seen in over a year. The money was a lifeline, a means to provide them with the comforts he had been unable to afford before.

As Rajesh made his way to the construction site, he couldn't help but feel a pang of longing for the familiar sights and sounds of his hometown. He missed the gentle breeze rustling through the mango trees, the lively chatter of his neighbours, and the warm embrace of his family. But those memories were now filled with a sense of guilt, for he knew that his sacrifice had come at a great personal cost.

The work on the construction site was tiresome, with Rajesh and his colleagues labouring under the scorching sun, their bodies aching from the physical strain. Rajesh often found himself daydreaming about his family, wondering how they were faring back home. Were his children thriving in their studies? Had his wife managed to make ends meet with the money he sent?

One afternoon, as Rajesh was taking a brief rest from the heat, his phone rang. Recognizing his wife's number, he answered with a mixture of excitement and tension.

"Rajesh, when are you going to send more money?" Meera's voice crackled through the line; her tone laced with impatience. "Arjun's tuition fees are due, and we need to pay for Aisha's dance lessons. You know how important it is for her to keep up with her peers."

Rajesh felt a familiar pang of guilt. "I'm doing my best, Meera," he replied, his voice weary. "The work has been slow, and the cost of living here is so high. But I'll try to send more as soon as I can."

"Try harder, Rajesh," Meera snapped. "You know how important it is for the children to have every opportunity. We can't let them fall behind."

Rajesh sighed, his shoulders weakened with the burden of life, "I understand, Meera. I'll do what I can."

As he ended the call, Rajesh felt a heaviness settle in his chest. The weight of his family's expectations was a constant burden, one that threatened to crush him under its unending demands. He knew that his sacrifice was necessary, but sometimes he couldn't help but wonder if it was all worth it.

With a deep breath, Rajesh consoled himself and returned to the construction site, his mind already turning to the next task at hand. He would continue to work tirelessly, pushing himself to the limit, all for the sake of his family's comfort and security. It was a price he was willing to pay, no matter the cost to his own well-being.

As the sun began to set, casting a warm glow over the bustling city, Rajesh couldn't help but feel a sense of longing. He yearned for the day when he could return home, to be reunited with his loved ones and to find the peace he so desperately craved. But for now, his path was clear - to keep pushing forward, to keep providing, and to never lose sight of the reason he had come to this foreign land in the first place.

It had been ten years since he visited home, so he decided to go on a vacation to see his dear ones. His children must have grown up. Since he didn't have a smart phone, he couldn't see them all those years.

Rajesh's heart raced with anticipation as the plane touched down on the runway of the small airport in his hometown. After over ten years of heavy labour in the Middle East, he was finally back home, eager to embrace his family once more. As he stepped out of the terminal, the warm, humid air enveloped him, a stark contrast to the arid desert he had grown accustomed to.

Taking a rickshaw, Rajesh felt a sense of nostalgia all over him. The bustling streets, the vibrant colours, and the friendly faces - it was all so comforting, a far cry from the dry and humid environment of the Middle East. As the rickshaw weaved through the narrow lanes, Rajesh's eyes scanned the familiar landmarks, his mind filled with memories of his childhood. His hometown had a drastic change. The familiar landmarks have changed into strange sights.

After an hour's journey, the rickshaw pulled up in front of his home. It was now a huge mansion unlike the modest home it used to be ten years ago. Rajesh took a deep breath, his excitement to see how great his house looked and he took pride on its grand looks; after all it was his sweat that turned into a heaven like house. He had been away for so long, and he couldn't help but wonder how his family had changed in his absence.

Stepping through the gate, Rajesh was immediately greeted by the sight of his adolescent children, Arjun and Aisha, running towards him, their faces lit up with joy. "Baba!" they cried, enveloping him in a tight embrace. Rajesh felt his heart swell with love as he held them close, enjoying the moment.

Meera, his wife, emerged from the house, a warm smile on her face. "Welcome back, Rajesh," she said, her tone polite but distant. Rajesh noticed that her appearance had changed - she was dressed in a designer sari, her jewellery glittering in the afternoon sun. He couldn't help but feel a sense of unease, sensing a shift in the overall change of his household.

The children and his wife were so eager to see what he bought for them, but they were not happy to see that he bought only day to day items like soaps, perfumes, dishwash gel and so on. They were expecting him to bring latest gadgets and branded beauty products. This saddened him. He recollected how much he struggled to save and amass things one by one when the offers were there. But now his family seemed to have no value of the things he brought.

Over the next few days, Rajesh slowly settled back into the familiar surroundings of his home. However, as he spent more time with his family, he couldn't help but notice the stark contrast between their lifestyle and his own. While he had been living in a crowded shared room and subsisting on a meagre diet, his family had been enjoying a life of immense luxury.

The house had been renovated, and Rajesh marvelled at the new furniture and appliances that adorned the rooms. Arjun and Aisha were attending a prestigious private school, and Meera seemed to have a collection of expensive saris and jewellery. Rajesh couldn't help but feel a sense of unease, wondering how his family had managed to afford such extravagance while they often complained about not having sufficient money for the living.

One evening, as the family gathered for dinner, Rajesh brought in the subject. "Meera, I've noticed that the house has been renovated and the children are attending a new school. How have you been managing all of this?"

Meera's eyes narrowed, and Rajesh could sense the defensiveness in her tone. "Well, Rajesh, you've been away for so long, and the children's education is important. We've had to make some adjustments to ensure they have the best opportunities."

Arjun, who had been silent until this point, chimed in. "Yes, Baba, the school is amazing. They have all the latest facilities, and the teachers are of high standard. I'm sure you can understand the importance of investing in our future."

Rajesh felt a pang of guilt, realizing that his absence had allowed his family to become accustomed to a lifestyle he could not fully provide for. "But Meera, I've been working hard, sending money back home every month. Surely, that should have been enough to cover the basic expenses?"

Meera's expression hardened. "Basic expenses? Rajesh, you've been away for over ten years. Do you have any idea how much the cost of living has gone up? The children need to keep up with their peers, and I have my own needs as well."

Rajesh felt a pain at his heart as he listened to Meera's words. He had sacrificed so much, working tirelessly in the Middle East, only to have his efforts dismissed and his family's needs seem never ending. Suddenly, the lavish surroundings that had once filled him with pride now felt like a heavy burden.

As the dinner progressed, the conversation grew tense, with Arjun and Meera repeatedly emphasizing the importance of their lifestyle and the need for more financial support from Rajesh. Rajesh sat in silence, his heart sinking with each passing moment, feeling increasingly disconnected from the very people he had worked so hard to provide for.

By the time the meal had ended, Rajesh felt exhausted, both physically and emotionally. He retreated to the comfort of his old room, where he had spent countless nights dreaming of this moment. But now, instead of the joyful homecoming he had envisioned, he was left with a deep sense of unease and a growing realization that his sacrifice may have been in vain.

The news hit Rajesh like a thunderbolt, shattering the little peace he had managed to maintain during his homecoming. As he sat across the dining table from his family, the words spilled out about his job loss in the Middle East.

"I've lost my job," he said, his voice barely above a whisper. "The company had to let go of many workers due to the economic recession."

Meera's eyes widened, her manicured fingers gripping the edge of the table. "What do you mean, you've lost your job?" she demanded, her tone laced with a mixture of disbelief and anger. "How are we supposed to pay for Arjun's tuition fees and Aisha's piano lessons now?"

Rajesh bowed his head, the weight of his family's expectations pressing down on him. "I'm not sure," he admitted, his gaze falling to the floor.

Arjun, who had been silent until now, slammed his fist on the table, causing the cutlery to rattle. "This is unacceptable, Father," he said, his voice laced with disappointment. "You've been away for so long, and now you come back with nothing?"

Aisha, sensing the tension, reached out to touch Rajesh's arm, her eyes filled with concern. "But, Papa, what will we do?" she asked, her voice trembling.

Rajesh's heart sank as he watched his family's reactions unfold. The very people he had sacrificed so much for now seemed to care only about the material comforts they had grown accustomed to. He had hoped that his homecoming would be a time of reconnection and appreciation, but instead, it had become a battlefield of expectations and disappointment.

Meera's voice cut through the silence, her words dripping with accusation. "If you had just worked harder, Rajesh, we wouldn't be in this situation. But no, you had to come back and spoil our lives with your failure."

Rajesh felt the familiar sting of guilt and shame, his shoulders bowing under the weight of his family's judgment. "I'm sorry," he murmured, unable to meet their gaze. "I never meant for this to happen."

The tension in the room was palpable, and Rajesh could feel the distance growing between him and his family. He had given everything to provide for them, and now, in their hour of need, they turned their backs on him, unwilling to understand the sacrifices he had made.

Arjun, his eyes blazing with frustration, leaned forward, his finger pointing accusingly at Rajesh. "You've let us down, Father. All these years of hard work, and for what? We will be back to nothing now and it's all because of you."

Rajesh felt the weight of his family's disappointment at his heart. He had hoped that his return would bring them closer, but instead, it had only served to highlight the widened gap that had grown between them.

Meera's voice, now laced with scorn cut through the silence. "I think it's best if you leave, Rajesh. We can't have you dragging us down with your failures."

Rajesh's heart sank, the words cutting him like a knife. He had given everything for this family, and now they were discarding him like a used curry leaf. Tears stung his eyes, but he refused to let them fall, unwilling to show his family the depth of his pain.

"Very well," he said, his voice barely audible. "I'll leave, but know that I've always done my best to provide for you all."

As he rose from the table, Rajesh felt a sense of understanding wash over him. This was the end of a chapter, a painful realization that his sacrifices had not been enough to earn him a place in the hearts of those he loved the most. With a heavy heart, he turned and walked out the door, his footsteps echoing in the silence that followed.

Rajesh was feeling utterly rejected and abandoned, his dreams of a joyful homecoming shattered by the harsh reality of his family's selfishness and lack of appreciation. The emotional turmoil he experienced left him feeling lost and uncertain about his future, a far cry from the determined and resilient man he had been when he left for the Middle East. He took all what he had in a suitcase and left the house. No one was there to send him off, no one cared to know even where he would go.

Rajesh sat in the small, rented room, staring at the envelope in his hands. The severance package from his former employer in the Middle East had arrived, and the numbers on the check were far greater than what he expected. After the emotional conflict with his family and being mercilessly kicked out of his own home, this unexpected financial gain felt like a lifeline, a chance to start anew.

Carefully folding the check, Rajesh slipped it into his shirt pocket, his mind racing with possibilities. For years, he had sacrificed his own dreams and desires, pouring every ounce of his energy into providing for his family. But now, with this newfound financial security, he could finally focus on his own well-being, free from the constant pressure and demands of his loved ones.

Rajesh stood up, his shoulders no longer weighed down by the burden of expectations. He gazed out the window, taking in the familiar sights of his small hometown. The bustling streets, the vibrant colours, and the warm, friendly faces – all of it felt like a distant memory, a life he had once known. But now, with this severance package, he had the opportunity to rediscover himself, to embrace the freedom he had so long been denied.

Without hesitation, Rajesh packed his meagre belongings and checked out of the room. As he stepped out into the sunlight, he felt a sense of liberation wash over him. No longer beholden to his family's demands, he could design his life the way he wanted, explore his passions, and find the joy he had once known, years before during his single life.

Rajesh's first stop was the local market, where he wandered through the stalls, his senses awakened by the aromas of spices and the vibrant displays of fresh produce. He had always loved cooking, but his responsibilities had often forced him to rely on quick, affordable meals. Now, with the financial freedom, he could indulge in his culinary curiosities, experimenting with new ingredients and techniques.

As he strolled through the market, Rajesh struck up conversations with the vendors, learning about their stories and the local cuisine. He found himself drawn to a stall selling an array of exotic spices, and with a newfound enthusiasm, he began to gather the ingredients for a traditional Indian dish he had long forgotten.

With his basket full, Rajesh made his way to a small, secluded park on the outskirts of town. Nestled among the lush greenery, he set up an area to cook, carefully preparing the dish he had chosen. The familiar scents of cumin, coriander, and turmeric filled the air, and as he tasted the final product, a sense of contentment washed over him.

For the first time in years, Rajesh felt truly alive, free from the constant demands and expectations that had weighed him down. He savoured each bite, relishing the flavours and the simple pleasure of creating something for himself, without the pressure of pleasing others.

As the sun began to set, Rajesh packed up his cooking equipment and wandered deeper into the park. He found a secluded spot, a small clearing surrounded by towering trees, and settled down on the grass, watching the sky transform into a breathtaking canvas of oranges and pinks.

In this moment of solitude, Rajesh allowed himself to reflect on his past, the sacrifices he had made, and the toll it had taken on his own well-being. He had always believed that his duty to his family was paramount, that his own happiness was secondary to their needs. But now, as he sat in the tranquillity of the park, he realized that he had been living a life that was not truly his own.

Rajesh closed his eyes, taking a deep breath, and felt a sense of peace wash over him. He had been given a second chance, an opportunity to rediscover himself and find the joy he had long been denied. With a renewed sense of purpose, he opened his eyes, determined to embrace this new chapter of his life and create a future that was truly his own.

As the last rays of the sun dipped below the horizon, Rajesh stood up, his steps lighter and his spirit buoyed by the realization that he was no longer bound by the expectations of others. He had taken the first step towards reclaiming his life, and the journey ahead was filled with endless possibilities. He bought a second-hand traveller and renovated it into a mini caravan home. He always wanted to make a tour to all the famous spots of India, covering all the states, enjoying their cuisines and now it is the time for that. Rajesh found joy in his independence, creating a fulfilling life that values personal happiness over materialism. He reconciles with his past letting go of resentment toward his family and embraces the freedom that comes with his new life...

CHAPTER FOURTEEN

RESILIENCE IN REFLECTION

The warm afternoon sun streamed through the large windows of the bustling university library, casting a soft glow over the rows of bookshelves and the clusters of students engrossed in their studies. Amidst the hum of hushed conversations and the occasional rustling of pages, a young woman named Aisha sat at a table, her fingers gracefully turning the pages of an open textbook.

At 21 years old, Aisha was a beacon of kindness and compassion at the college campus. With her warm smile and gentle demeanour, she had quickly endeared herself to her peers, becoming a beloved figure in the community. Her academic excellence was matched only by her genuine concern for the well-being of those around her, and she often found herself lending a helping hand to her fellow students, whether it was tutoring a struggling classmate or organizing fundraisers for local charities.

As Aisha studied, her best friend Maya sat down in the chair beside her, a mischievous grin on her face. "Hey, there you are! I've been looking all over for you," Maya said, playfully pinching Aisha's arm.

Aisha looked up from her book, her dark eyes sparkling with amusement. "I should have known you'd find me here. Where else would I be?" she replied, her voice warm and melodic.

Maya laughed, "Well, I was hoping you'd be out enjoying the beautiful day instead of being lost in a book. Come on, let's go, grab some lunch!"

Aisha glanced at the clock, then back at her friend. "Alright, you've convinced me. I will take a break." She closed her textbook and gathered her belongings, following Maya out of the library and into the vibrant campus.

As they walked, Aisha couldn't help but notice the admiring glances that followed her. She had always been aware of her striking beauty, with her flawless skin, high cheekbones, and long, dark hair, but she never let it define her. To Aisha, her looks were simply a part of who she was, not the sum total of her worth.

The two friends made their way to a cozy cafe near the centre of campus, their laughter and easy chitchats filling the air around them. Aisha listened intently as Maya recounted the latest drama unfolding among them, her eyes sparkling with amusement.

Maya asked Aisha, "How are you doing by the way? Have any exciting plans for the weekend?"

Aisha paused, considering the question. "Nothing too exciting, really. I was thinking of volunteering at the care home again, and maybe doing some help in the community kitchen. You know how much I love to be around the inmates. They remind me of my late grandparents."

Maya nodded, her expression softening. "That sounds perfect. You always manage to find ways to make a difference, don't you?" She reached across the table and gave Aisha's hand a gentle squeeze.

Aisha smiled warmly, her heart swelling with gratitude for her best friend's unwavering support. "I just want to do what I can to help others, you know? Even if it's in small ways."

As the two young women continued their conversation, without their knowledge, a pair of intense eyes was watching their every move. Rahul, a 23-year-old student with a troubled past, had been captivated by Aisha from the moment he first laid eyes on her. His obsession had only grown stronger over time, fuelled by a deep-seated jealousy.

Rahul's gaze followed Aisha as she and Maya left the cafe, his fingers tightening around the cup of coffee he held. He knew he couldn't keep his feelings hidden forever, but the thought of Aisha rejecting him filled him with a sense of dread and rage. In his mind, she belonged to him, and he would stop at nothing to make her his own.

As the sun began to set over the crowded campus, Aisha and Maya returned to their hostel, their laughter a stark contrast to the dark thoughts brewing in Rahul's mind. Little did they know that their world was about to be shattered by what was about to unfold.

The afternoon sun streamed through the library windows, casting a warm glow over the bustling campus. Aisha sat at her usual study area, her fingers gliding across the keyboard as she typed fast determined to finish her research paper before the weekend. Lost in her work, she didn't notice Rahul's intense gaze following her every move from across the room.

Rahul had been infatuated with Aisha since the first day he'd laid eyes on her. Her radiant smile, her kind demeanour, and her unwavering commitment to helping others - it all fuelled his obsession. He had tried numerous times to approach her, to strike up a conversation, but Aisha had always politely escaped his advances, unaware of the growing darkness in Rahul's heart.

In the afternoon, Rahul gathered all the courage to make his move. He came over to Aisha's table, @Hey, Aisha. I couldn't help but notice you sitting here all alone. Why don't you take a break and join me for coffee?"

Aisha looked up, shocked by his sudden presence. "Oh, hi Rahul. I appreciate the offer, but I really need to finish this paper. Maybe another time?" She gave him a warm smile, hoping to avoid the situation.

Rahul's jaw tightened, his eyes narrowing, "Come on, Aisha. You're always working so hard. You deserve a little break. I promise I'll make it worth your while." He leaned in, his voice lowering to a near-whisper.

Aisha shifted uncomfortably in her seat, her heart racing. "I'm sorry, Rahul, but I really can't. I have a lot to do, and I don't want to fall behind." She gathered her books, preparing to leave.

Rahul's expression darkened, he gripped the edge of the table, "You're always making excuses, Aisha. Why can't you just give me a chance?" His voice rose, drawing the attention of nearby students.

Aisha stood up, her hands trembling. "Rahul, please, I'm not interested. I think it's best if we just go our separate ways." She turned to leave, but Rahul's hand shot out, grabbing her arm.

"You're not going anywhere until you listen to me!" he hissed, his grip tightening.

Aisha cried in pain, her eyes wide with fear. "Let go of me, Rahul! You're hurting me!" she cried, drawing the attention of the librarian.

Before Aisha could react, Rahul's other hand reached into his backpack, pulling out a small bottle. "If I can't have you, no one will!" he shouted, uncapping the bottle and throwing the contents at Aisha's face. She screamed in agony, the burning sensation overwhelming her senses. Chaos erupted in the library as students scattered, some rushing to Aisha's aid while others fled in terror.

Maya, who had been studying in a nearby nook, heard the commotion and rushed to her friend's side. "Aisha! Oh my God, what happened?" she cried, her hands trembling as she tried to help.

Aisha's face was burning, her skin blistering and peeling away. "Rahul... he attacked me," she managed to tell out between agonizing cries.

The library was in terror calling emergency services and bystanders trying to aid. Rahul stood frozen, the empty bottle still clutched in his hand, his expression a mixture of horror and disbelief.

As the sirens wailed in the distance, Aisha's world faded to black, the agonizing pain overwhelming her senses. The last thing she heard was Maya's terrified voice, begging her to hold on.

Aisha's eyes fluttered open, the harsh fluorescent lights of the hospital ward assaulting her senses. The familiar faces of her parents and Maya came into focus, their expressions filled with worry and disbelief. As the fog in her mind slowly cleared, the memories of the attack came rushing back, and Aisha's heart raced with a mix of fear and confusion.

"Aisha, my child, you're safe now," her mother said, gently patting her hand, "The doctors say you're going to be okay."

Aisha's eyes instinctively darted to the bandages covering the left side of her face, a painful reminder of the trauma she had endured. She winced, the throbbing pain a constant companion. Maya leaned in, her eyes brimming with tears.

"I'm so sorry, Aisha. I should have been there with you," she whispered, her voice laced with guilt.

Aisha gave in a weak smile, her own eyes welled up, "It's not your fault, Maya. None of this is your fault."

In the days that followed, Aisha's recovery became a painful battle, both physically and emotionally. The doctors worked tirelessly to treat her burns, performing delicate procedures to minimize scarring. Each session was a test of Aisha's resilience, as she gritted her teeth through the pain and discomfort.

But the true challenge lay in her mental and emotional healing. Aisha found herself struggling to come to terms with her new appearance, the once vibrant and confident young woman now in now covered in doubt and insecurity. She avoided mirrors, afraid to confront the reflection that stared back at her.

Maya remained a constant source of support, accompanying Aisha to her therapy sessions with Dr. Patel, a compassionate and experienced counsellor. In the quiet solace of the therapist's office, Aisha began to unpack the layers of her trauma, sharing her fears and doubts.

"It's understandable to feel this way, Aisha," Dr. Patel said, her voice soothing. "What you've been through is a profound and life-altering experience. But I want you to know that your worth is not defined by your appearance", said the doctor.

Aisha listened intently; her brow furrowed in concentration. "But how can I feel beautiful again, when I can barely look at myself in the mirror?"

Dr. Patel offered a gentle smile. "Beauty is not just skin-deep. It's about the light that shines from within you – your kindness, your compassion, your resilience. Those are the qualities that make you truly beautiful, Aisha."

Slowly, with the support of her therapist and her unwavering friend, Aisha began to rediscover the strength that had always been a part of her. She started to challenge the negative thoughts that threatened to consume her, reminding herself of the positive impact she had on those around her.

One day, as Aisha sat in the hospital garden, she caught a glimpse of her reflection in a window. She paused, taking a deep breath, and allowed herself to truly look. The scars were still raw and angry, but Aisha saw beyond them, recognizing the resilience and determination in her eyes.

"I am more than this," she whispered to herself, a newfound resolve taking hold.

Aisha's progress, though gradual, was undeniable. She began to participate in support groups, sharing her story with others who had faced similar challenges. The vulnerability she displayed, coupled with her unwavering spirit, inspired those around her, reminding them that true beauty transcends the physical.

As the days turned into weeks, Aisha's confidence grew, and she found herself embracing her scars as a testament to her strength. She started to explore her creative passions, immersing herself in drawing and painting, using art as a means of self-expression and healing.

One evening, as Aisha sat in her dorm room, surrounded by her vibrant sketches, Maya entered with a determined look on her face.

"Aisha, I know you've been through so much, but I think it's time for you to share your story with the world," she said, her voice firm yet encouraging.

Aisha's heart raced, a mixture of fear and anticipation. "I'm not sure I'm ready, Maya. What if people don't understand?"

Maya reached out and squeezed Aisha's hand. "Aisha, you are so much more than your scars. Your story has the power to inspire others, to challenge the way we view beauty. And I know you're ready to share that with the world."

Aisha considered her friend's words, a flicker of hope igniting within her. Perhaps, in sharing her journey, she could help others find the courage to embrace their own beauty, regardless of what the world might say.

With a deep breath, Aisha nodded, a newfound determination etched on her face. "Okay, let's do it."

As she prepared to take the stage and share her story, Aisha knew that the road ahead would not be easy, but she was no longer alone. With the support of her loved ones and the strength she had discovered within herself, she was ready to redefine the meaning of true beauty.

Aisha stared at her reflection, tracing the uneven contours of her scarred face with a trembling hand. The once vibrant, youthful features she had taken for granted were now a stark reminder of the trauma she had endured. Rahul's violent attack had shattered more than just her skin; it had shaken the very foundation of her self-confidence.

As she sat in Dr. Patel's office, the experienced therapist's soothing voice guided her through the emotional turmoil, "Aisha, your scars do not define you. They are a testament to your resilience, a symbol of the strength you've cultivated within."

Aisha nodded slowly, her eyes brimming with tears, "I know, Dr. Patel, but it's so hard to see past them. Everyone looks at me differently now, like I'm some sort of fragile, broken thing."

Dr. Patel leaned forward, her gaze unwavering. "The only person who can change that perception is you. You have the power to redefine beauty, to show the world that true worth lies not in physical appearance, but in the depths of one's character."

Aisha's breath caught in her throat as the weight of those words sank in. For weeks, she had been consumed by self-doubt, hiding behind layers of makeup and scarves, desperately trying to conceal the changes to her face. But now, a glimmer of determination began to flicker within her.

"You're right," she said, her voice steadier than it had been in months. "I can't let Rahul's actions dictate how I see myself. I won't let him take away my power."

Dr. Patel smiled, her eyes shining with pride. "That's the Aisha I know. Now, let's talk about how you can share your story and inspire others who have faced similar challenges."

As Aisha left the therapy session, she felt a newfound sense of purpose. Rahul's obsession had nearly destroyed her, but she refused to let him win. With Maya's unwavering support and Dr. Patel's guidance, Aisha began to plan her next steps.

In the days that followed, Aisha poured her heart into crafting her speech, determined to use her experience to challenge societal perceptions of beauty. She wanted to show the world that scars could be symbols of resilience, not shame.

The day of the event, Aisha's palms were sweaty, and her heart raced with a mixture of nerves and anticipation. As she stepped onto the stage, she scanned the audience, finding the familiar faces of her loved ones – Maya, her parents, and even Dr. Patel – offering silent encouragement.

Aisha took a deep breath and began to speak, her voice steady and confident. "When I look in the mirror, I see a survivor. I see someone who has endured unimaginable pain, but who has emerged stronger, more resilient than ever before."

The audience listened in complete silence as Aisha shared her story, her words painting a vivid picture of the trauma she had faced and the journey of self-acceptance she had carried upon.

"Rahul's actions robbed me of my physical beauty, but they could not take away my inner strength. I am more than the scars on my face; I am a person of compassion, intelligence, and unwavering determination."

Aisha paused, her gaze sweeping across the crowd. She continued, "We live in a world that values physical perfection above all else, but I am here to tell you that true beauty lies within. It is the kindness we show to others, the passions we pursue, and the resilience we demonstrate in the face of adversity."

As Aisha spoke, the audience erupted in thunderous applause, their eyes shining with tears of empathy and admiration. Maya beamed with pride, while Dr. Patel nodded approvingly, her expression radiating a sense of accomplishment.

In that moment, Aisha felt a weight lift from her shoulders. She had reclaimed her power, her voice, and her sense of self-worth. No longer would she hide behind layers of concealment; instead, she would embrace her scars as a testament to her strength and resilience.

As the event drew to a close, Aisha was surrounded by a crowd of well-wishers, each person eager to express their gratitude and support. She listened intently, her heart swelling with a newfound sense of purpose.

"I'm not done yet," Aisha thought to herself, a determined gleam in her eyes. "This is just the beginning. I will use my voice to empower others, to show them that they are more than the sum of their physical attributes."

With a renewed sense of conviction, Aisha knew that her journey of self-acceptance was only the first step in a larger mission – to redefine the very notion of beauty, one story at a time.

CHAPTER FIFTEEN

BEHIND THE SPOTLIGHT - A FIGHT FOR RECOGNITION

The film set was a rollercoaster of activities, with crew members running about and cameras capturing every moment. Arjun stood amidst the chaos, ready for action, waiting for his turn. As the director called for a stunt sequence, Arjun sprung into motion, his movements fluid and precise, defying gravity with each leap and tumble.

Yet, despite his exceptional skills, Arjun often felt like an invisible person in the film field as the action is done by him, but the credit goes to the lead actor. The director, Rohan, shouted orders, his eyes fixed on the lead actors, while Arjun's contributions were brushed aside, his talents unappreciated. Arjun tightened his jaw, swallowing the frustration that threatened to boil over.

Across the set, Meera stood in the background, her eyes trained on the lead dancer, absorbing every step and sway. As a background dancer, her role was often overlooked, her skills overshadowed by the stars. Still, Meera poured her heart into every performance, driven by a deep-rooted passion for dance.

Meera's self-respect was shattered when a crew member, with his filthy stench of alcohol, stumbled past her, "Hey, sweetheart, why don't you shake that pretty little thing for me?" he slurred, his gaze lingering on her body.

Meera's stomach churned, and she instinctively took a step back, her face flushing with a mixture of embarrassment and fear. The crew member chuckled, his laughter echoing across the set, drawing the attention of a few nearby artists.

Arjun, who had been watching the interaction from the corner of his eye, felt a surge of anger. He strode towards the crew member, his brow furrowed, "That's enough," he said, his voice firm. "Leave her alone."

The crew member turned, his expression shifting from amusement to annoyance. He yelled, "What's your problem, man? I was just having a little fun." He sneered, his gaze sweeping over Meera.

Arjun stepped between them, shielding Meera from the crew member's leering eyes. Arjun stated, "This isn't fun. It's harassment, and it needs to stop."

The crew member scoffed, rolling his eyes and said, "Oh, come on, don't be such a killjoy. These girls are here to entertain us, aren't they?" He gestured towards Meera, who shrunk back, her arms wrapped protectively around herself.

Arjun's jaw tightened, and he opened his mouth to retort, but before he could, Rohan's voice boomed across the set, "What's going on here? We're on a tight schedule, people. Let's get back to work!"

The crew member shot Arjun a defiant glare and slinked away, leaving Arjun and Meera standing in the tense silence. Meera's eyes were downcast, her shoulders hunched, and Arjun felt a pang of empathy.

Hesitantly, he placed a hand on Meera's arm, drawing her attention. "Are you okay?" he asked, his voice low and gentle.

Meera lifted her gaze, her eyes glistening with unshed tears. "I'm fine," she murmured, her voice barely above a whisper. "It's not the first time something like this has happened."

Arjun's heart sank, and he felt a surge of protectiveness towards this young woman who had been forced to endure such blatant disrespect. "That's not right," he said, his tone resolute. "You shouldn't have to put up with this."

Meera offered him a small, weary smile and said, “It's just the way things are, I guess. We're the invisible ones, the ones who don't matter."

Arjun shook his head, his determination growing and remarked, "Well, that's going to change. I won't stand by and watch this happen anymore."

Meera's eyes widened, and for a moment, a glimmer of hope flickered across her features. "You mean that?" she asked, her voice tinged with disbelief.

Arjun nodded; his gaze unwavering. "Yes, I do. We're going to do something about this, Meera. Together."

The two artists stood there, united in their shared struggle, their bond forged in the face of adversity. As the chaos of the film set swirled around them, Arjun and Meera knew that their fight was just beginning, but they were ready to take a stand against the industry's toxic culture.

The bustling energy of the film set had a way of masking the underlying tensions that simmered beneath the surface. Arjun observed the scene, his eyes scanning the crowd of crew members as they scurried about, focused on their tasks. But his gaze kept returning to Meera, the young dancer whose delicate frame seemed to shrink with each passing moment.

After witnessing the harassment she had faced the previous day, Arjun felt a sense of unease that refused to dissipate. He knew all too well the challenges junior artists like Meera faced, the constant struggle for recognition and respect. It was a battle he had been fighting for years, albeit with little success.

As the day wore on, Arjun found himself gravitating towards Meera, drawn to the vulnerability that shone through her determined demeanour. During a break, he approached her cautiously, offering a sympathetic ear.

"Hey, how are you holding up?" Arjun asked, his voice low and gentle.

Meera's eyes darted around, as if afraid of being overheard. "I'm... I'm doing okay, I guess," she replied, her words laced with uncertainty.

Arjun could see the strain etched on her face, the way her fingers trembled slightly. He said, "Look, about what happened yesterday, I'm sorry you had to go through that. It's not right, and it shouldn't be brushed aside as a joke."

Meera's gaze met his, a flicker of relief washing over her features. She said, "I'm glad someone else sees it that way. The others, they just laugh it off, like it's no big deal. But it is a big deal, you know? We're not just props, we're human beings."

Arjun nodded, his heart aching for the young woman before him. He said, "Exactly. And its high time the industry starts treating us like it. I've been trying to speak up for years, but it's always fallen on deaf ears."

A spark of determination ignited in Meera's eyes. With a sigh of affirmation she said, "Maybe it's time we do something about it, then. Together."

Arjun felt a surge of hope at her words and replied, "I'm with you, Meera. We can't let this keep happening, not to you or anyone else."

As they discussed their shared experiences and brainstormed ways to confront the toxic culture, Arjun couldn't help but admire Meera's resilience. Despite the constant barrage of harassment, she refused to be broken, her spirit still burning bright.

The following days saw their bond deepen, as they confided in each other about the challenges they faced. Meera opened up about the constant self-doubt that plagued her, the way the industry's dismissive attitude had chipped away at her self-worth. Arjun, in turn, shared his frustrations with the lack of recognition for his skills, the way the director, Rohan, had repeatedly overlooked him in favour of more "marketable" performers.

Their conversations were a delicate dance, a careful balance of vulnerability and determination. They knew that speaking out against the system would come at a cost, but the desire to create change burned brighter than their fears.

One day, as they rehearsed a particularly demanding stunt sequence, Meera found herself on the receiving end of another unsettling encounter. A crew member, emboldened by the lax attitudes of his colleagues, made a lewd comment about her appearance, his gaze lingering in a way that made her skin crawl.

Meera's heart raced, her hands trembling as she tried to maintain her composure. Arjun, ever vigilant, noticed the shift in her demeanour immediately. He quickly stepped in, his voice firm and unwavering.

"Hey, that's not okay. Keep your comments to yourself and focus on the work, yeah?" Arjun's words were laced with a barely contained fury, his protective instincts kicking in.

The crew member scoffed, his eyes narrowing told him, "Relax, man. It was just a joke. You're too sensitive."

Arjun's jaw clenched, his fists balling at his sides and asked, "A joke? This isn't a joke, its harassment, and I won't stand for it. Meera deserves to be treated with respect, just like the rest of us."

The tension in the air was palpable, the other crew members falling silent as they witnessed the confrontation. Meera's gaze darted between the two men, her heart pounding in her chest.

Rohan, the director, finally stepped in, his voice sharp and authoritative shouted, "Alright, that's enough. Let's get back to work, people. We've got a film to finish."

Arjun shot Rohan a pointed look, his frustration evident and replied, "This isn't over, Rohan. We need to talk about the way junior artists are treated on this set."

Rohan's expression hardened, a clear warning in his eyes and said, "We can discuss it later. Right now, I need everyone focused on their jobs."

As the crew resumed their tasks, Arjun turned to Meera, his features softening asked, "Are you okay?" he asked, his voice laced with concern.

Meera nodded, her eyes glistening with unshed tears she replied, "I am, thanks to you. But I can't keep living like this, Arjun. Something needs to change."

Arjun placed a gentle hand on her shoulder, his resolve strengthening. He replied, "I know, Meera. And we're going to make sure it does. Together."

The tension on set had been palpable ever since Arjun's confrontation with the crew member over Meera's harassment. Meera could feel the hostile glares and whispers directed her way, as if she had committed some unforgivable sin by standing up for herself. But with Arjun by her side, she found the courage to keep her head held high.

One afternoon, as the crew prepared for a particularly demanding stunt sequence, Arjun approached Meera, his brow furrowed with determination, "Meera, I think it's time we take this to the next level. We can't keep letting these incidents slide. We need to report what's been happening."

Meera's heart raced at the prospect, "But what if they retaliate? I can't afford to lose this job, Arjun. My family is counting on me."

Arjun placed a reassuring hand on her shoulder, "I know it's risky, but staying silent won't change anything. We must be the ones to break the cycle of abuse. I'll be right here with you, every step of the way."

Mustering her courage, Meera nodded, "Okay, let's do it."

Together, they approached the production manager, their voices trembling but resolute as they recounted the incidents of harassment. To their dismay, the manager brushed off their concerns, dismissing the incidents as "harmless fun" and warning them against jeopardizing the film's completion.

Undeterred, Arjun and Meera turned to social media, determined to amplify their voices and rally support from their peers. They began sharing their stories, detailing the toxic culture that had become the norm in the industry. To their surprise, their posts quickly gained traction, with fellow junior artists reaching out to share their own harrowing experiences.

One such artist was Leela, a shy but talented background dancer who had witnessed Meera's harassment firsthand. Hesitantly, she approached Arjun and Meera, her eyes filled with a mixture of fear and admiration.

"I...I saw what happened to you, Meera," Leela stammered. "I want to help, but I'm so scared of the consequences. What if they blacklist me?"

Arjun placed a reassuring hand on Leela's arm, "We understand your fear, Leela. But the only way to create change is to stand together. Your voice matters, and together, we can make a difference."

Meera nodded in agreement, "Arjun's right. We're in this fight together. If you're willing, we'd be honoured to have you join us."

Leela's eyes widened, and after a moment of contemplation, she nodded resolutely, "Okay, I'll do it. I'm tired of being invisible and afraid. It's time to speak out."

With Leela's addition to their team, Arjun and Meera's social media campaign gained even more momentum. They shared personal accounts, heartbreaking testimonies, and calls to action, urging the industry to address the systemic issues that had long been swept under the rug.

The response was overwhelming. Thousands of junior artists, both on set and across the country, began sharing their own stories, lending their voices to the growing movement. Suddenly, the issue of harassment and exploitation was no longer a whispered secret, but a roar that could no longer be ignored.

Rohan, the director, grew increasingly agitated as the public outcry escalated. During a tense confrontation on set, he cornered Arjun, his eyes burning with fury.

"This little crusade of yours is jeopardizing my film," Rohan spat. "If you don't shut it down immediately, I'll make sure you never work in this industry again."

Arjun stood his ground, unwavering in the face of Rohan's threats, "I'm not the one jeopardizing anything, Rohan. You and your crew are the ones who have been exploiting and abusing junior artists for far too long. It's time for that to end."

Rohan's lips curled into a sneer. "You think you can just waltz in and change the way things are done? This is my set, my vision. You're nothing but a disposable cog in the machine. Remember that."

As Rohan stormed off, Arjun felt a surge of determination. He knew that the road ahead would be arduous, but he was more convinced than ever that the fight was worth it. With Meera and Leela by his side, he was ready to take on the industry's titans and demand the change that junior artists so desperately needed.

The chapter concluded with Arjun, Meera, and Leela huddled together, their eyes filled with a newfound resolve. They had taken the first steps towards a revolution, and they were prepared to face the consequences, no matter how daunting they might be.

The streets of Mumbai buzzed with energy as the city prepared for the prestigious Bollywood awards ceremony. Amidst the glitz and glamour, a different kind of movement was gaining momentum – one that sought to challenge the industry's deep-rooted issues of exploitation and harassment.

Arjun and Meera stood at the forefront of this growing campaign, their once-overlooked voices now echoing through the halls of power. The public outcry sparked by their social media exposé had reverberated across the nation, shattering the industry's veneer of perfection.

As the trio – Arjun, Meera, and Leela – gathered in a dimly lit cafe, the air crackled with a sense of anticipation. They had come a long way from the silent sufferers they once were, now emboldened by the support of their peers and the unwavering determination to see their fight through.

"The rally is scheduled for tomorrow," Meera said, her fingers trembling slightly as she traced the rim of her cup,"I can't believe we've come this far. It's both exhilarating and terrifying."

Arjun reached across the table, giving her hand a reassuring squeeze. "We've weathered the storm together, Meera. Tomorrow, we'll stand united, and our voices will be heard."

Leela, who had once been timid and easily intimidated, now sat with a newfound confidence said, "I never imagined I'd be part of something so powerful. This is our chance to make a real difference, to ensure that no one else has to suffer the way we did."

The trio discussed the logistics of the rally, mapping out their strategy to maximize the impact of their message. They knew that the road ahead would not be easy, but the prospect of a safer, more equitable industry fuelled their determination.

As the day of the rally dawned, the streets of Mumbai were flooded with a sea of junior artists, each holding signs that bore the scars of their experiences. Arjun, Meera, and Leela stood at the forefront, their faces etched with a mix of nervousness and resolve.

Meera stepped up to the microphone, her voice trembling at first, but soon gaining strength as she shared her story. She stated, "For too long, we have been silenced, treated as invisible cogs in the machine of Bollywood. No more! We demand respect, we demand safety, and we demand a future where our talents are celebrated, not exploited."

The crowd erupted in thunderous applause, their collective voices echoing through the streets. Arjun followed, his words carrying the weight of his own struggles and the frustrations of countless others like him. Arjun remarked, "We are not just background dancers or stunt performers – we are artists, dreamers, and contributors to the magic that captivates audiences worldwide. Yet, our dreams have been overshadowed by a culture of abuse, where those in power seek to maintain their grip on the industry."

Leela, her once-timid demeanour now replaced by a fierce determination, added her voice to the chorus. She stated, "We stand here today, united in our refusal to accept this injustice. We will no longer be silenced, nor will we allow our colleagues to suffer in the shadows. This is our industry, and we will fight to reclaim it."

The rally continued, with speakers from all corners of the Bollywood community sharing their stories and rallying the crowd to action. As the sun began to set, the participants marched towards the prestigious awards ceremony, their chants echoing through the streets.

Arjun, Meera, and Leela found themselves at the centre of the movement, their faces illuminated by the flashing cameras of the media. For a moment, they basked in the recognition, a stark contrast to the days when they had been dismissed and overlooked.

As the awards ceremony commenced, the trio waited anxiously in the wings. To their surprise, the host paused the proceedings to acknowledge the ongoing rally, praising the bravery of the junior artists who had risked their careers to speak out.

"Tonight, we celebrate not only the achievements of our industry's stars, but also the unsung heroes – the dancers, the stunt performers, and the backbone of our beloved Bollywood. Without their dedication and passion, the magic we witness on the silver screen would not be possible."

The audience erupted in thunderous applause, and Arjun, Meera, and Leela found themselves being ushered onto the stage. As they stood before the glittering crowd, they knew that their fight had only just begun, but the tides were turning.

In that moment, they recognized that injustice should never be tolerated, and that the power of collective action could indeed bring about meaningful change. With renewed vigour, they vowed to continue their crusade, ensuring that the industry they loved would become a place of respect, safety, and equal opportunity for all.

CHAPTER SIXTEEN

BREAKING THE SILENCE -A TEACHER'S JOURNEY

Aditi Sharma took a deep breath as she stood before the ornated wooden doors of the international school. This was it - her first day as a teacher in a foreign country, a new chapter in her life. After years of honing her skills back home in India, she had embarked on this adventure, determined to make a fruitful career.

Aditi pushed open the doors and stepped into the bustling hallway. The air was filled with the chatter of students, their voices mingling in a symphony of different accents and languages. Aditi couldn't help but feel a twinge of nervousness as she made her way to the staff room, her heels clicking against the polished floors.

As she entered the staff room, Aditi was greeted by a sea of unfamiliar faces. She scanned the room, searching for a friendly smile, when a fellow teacher approached her.

"You must be the new English teacher," the woman said, extending her hand. "I'm Sarah, welcome to the team."

"It's a pleasure to meet you, Sarah," Aditi replied, shaking the woman's hand firmly. "I'm Aditi Sharma, and I'm excited to be here."

Sarah gave her an encouraging smile. "The students can be a handful, but I'm sure you'll do just fine. Let me show you to your classroom."

Aditi followed Sarah through the bustling hallways, her heart racing with a mixture of anticipation and trepidation. As they approached the door to her classroom, Aditi felt a surge of determination. This was her chance to make a difference, to inspire young minds and foster a love for learning.

"Well, here we are," Sarah said, gesturing to the door. "I'll leave you to get settled. The students will be arriving shortly."

"Thank you, Sarah," Aditi replied, her voice laced with a hint of nervousness. "I'm ready for this."

With a final nod, Sarah departed, leaving Aditi alone to face her new challenge. Aditi took a deep breath and pushed open the door, stepping into the spacious classroom. The desks were neatly arranged, and the walls were adorned with colourful posters and educational displays. Aditi ran her fingers along the smooth surface of the teacher's desk, a sense of pride swelling within her.

Moments later, the sound of chattering students filled the air as they began to file into the classroom. Aditi watched them with a mixture of excitement and trepidation, her eyes scanning the faces of her new students. She recognized the diversity in the room - a tapestry of cultures and backgrounds, each student a unique thread in the grand tapestry of the school.

As the students settled into their seats, Aditi stepped forward, her gaze sweeping across the room. "Good morning, class," she began, her voice clear and confident. "My name is Aditi and I'll be your English teacher this year."

A few students exchanged glances, and Aditi noticed a hint of indifference in their expressions. Undeterred, she continued, "I'm excited to get to know each and every one of you and to help you grow as students and individuals."

Aditi paused, her eyes settling on a young man sitting in the back row. He was slouched in his chair, his dark hair falling over his eyes, and a bored expression etched on his face. Aditi recognized him as Omer, the student whose name had been mentioned during her orientation.

"Omer, is it?" Aditi said, addressing the student directly. "I hope you're as excited about this year as I am."

Omer's eyes narrowed as he met Aditi's gaze, and a hint of a smirk tugged at the corners of his lips. "We'll see about that, Ms. Aditi," he drawled, his voice dripping with sarcasm.

Aditi felt a flicker of unease, but she refused to let it show. "Well, then, I look forward to proving you wrong," she replied, her tone firm yet warm.

The exchange did not go unnoticed by the other students, and Aditi could sense the shift in the classroom atmosphere. She knew she had her work cut out for her, but she was determined to win over her students, one by one.

As the class settled down, Aditi launched into her lesson, her passion for the subject shining through. She engaged the students, encouraging them to participate and share their thoughts. For a moment, she saw a glimmer of interest in their eyes, and she felt a surge of hope.

However, the moment was short-lived. Omer, who had been slouching in his chair, suddenly sat up, a mischievous grin on his face. "Hey, Ms. Aditi, how do you say 'respect' in your language?" he asked, his voice dripping with mockery.

The other students erupted in laughter, and Aditi felt her heart sink. She had known this would be a challenge, but the blatant disrespect from her students stung. Taking a deep breath, she met Omer's gaze, her expression unwavering.

"Respect is a universal language, Omer," she replied, her voice calm and measured. "And it's something I expect from all of my students, regardless of their background."

The laughter died down, and Aditi could see a flicker of surprise in Omer's eyes. She knew in that moment that this was just the beginning of a long and arduous journey, but she was determined to make a difference, one student at a time.

As the class came to an end, Aditi watched the students file out, her mind racing with a mixture of emotions. She had faced her first challenge, and while it had been difficult, she was more resolute than ever to prove her worth and earn the respect of her students.

With a deep breath, Aditi gathered her belongings and headed out of the classroom, her steps filled with a newfound determination. This was her chance to make a difference, and she was not about to let it slip away.

The morning bell rang, signalling the start of another day at the international school. Aditi Sharma took a deep breath, mentally preparing herself for the challenges that lay ahead. As she entered the classroom, she was met with the familiar sight of her students - some chatting amongst themselves, others scrolling through their phones, seemingly disengaged from the world around them.

Aditi cleared her throat, "Good morning, class. I hope you all had a restful weekend." She was greeted with a smattering of half-hearted responses, the students' attention still focused elsewhere.

Undeterred, Aditi launched into her lesson, determined to capture their interest. She spoke with passion, weaving in examples and anecdotes to illustrate the concepts. But as she turned to write on the board, she heard a snicker from the back of the room.

"Hey, Miss, can you please speak a little slower? I'm having trouble understanding your accent," Omer said, eliciting laughter from a few of his friends.

Aditi felt her cheeks flush, but she refused to let her composure falter. "Thank you for the feedback, Omer. I'll be sure to speak more clearly." She continued the lesson, but the disruptive behaviour only escalated.

Throughout the day, Aditi faced a barrage of disrespect from her students. They passed notes, threw paper airplanes, and openly challenged her instructions. Omer, in particular, seemed to take great pleasure in undermining her authority.

During a group activity, Aditi noticed Omer and his friends huddled together, giggling. As she approached them, she caught a glimpse of her own face drawn on a piece of paper, with exaggerated features and a speech bubble that read, "Can you please repeat that?"

Aditi felt a surge of anger, but she took a deep breath and addressed the class. "I understand that some of you may find my accent or teaching style unfamiliar, but I expect all of you to show respect in this classroom. Mocking me or disrupting the lesson is unacceptable."

Her words were met with a deafening silence, and Aditi could see the defiance in the students' eyes. Feeling defeated, she dismissed the class and retreated to the staff lounge, her heart heavy with frustration.

As Aditi sat alone, sipping a cup of lukewarm tea, a fellow teacher, Emma, approached her. "Hey, Aditi, I couldn't help but notice the commotion in your classroom earlier. Is everything alright?"

Aditi sighed, "To be honest, Emma, I'm struggling. The students here just don't seem to respect me. No matter what I do, they find ways to undermine my authority. Forget about respecting, they are mocking and mimicking me even."

Emma nodded sympathetically. "I remember when I first started teaching here. It can be tough, especially when you're an outsider. Have you tried talking to the administration about the issues you're facing?"

Aditi shook her head, "I did, but the principal just brushed me off. He said the students' satisfaction is the top priority, and that I need to find a way to better engage them."

Emma frowned, "That's not right. You're the expert in the classroom, and you deserve support. Have you considered trying some different teaching methods? Maybe something more interactive or hands-on?"

Aditi thought about it for a moment. "I have been trying to connect with them, but it's been an uphill battle. I just feel so isolated and unsure of myself sometimes." She paused, her gaze drifting to the window. "And then there's the financial pressure at home. I need this job, but it's becoming increasingly difficult to manage."

Emma reached out and squeezed Aditi's hand. "I know it's tough, but don't give up. You're a brilliant teacher, and I believe you can turn this around. Why don't you try talking to the students, really trying to understand where they're coming from?"

Aditi nodded, feeling a glimmer of hope. "You're right. I need to find a way to connect with them on a deeper level. Maybe that's the key to earning their respect."

As Aditi left the staff lounge, she couldn't shake the weight of the challenges she faced. But she was determined to find a way to break through the barriers and create a positive learning environment for her students. The road ahead would not be easy, but Aditi was more resolute than ever to make her mark in this classroom.

The morning bell rang, signalling the start of another day at the international school. Aditi Sharma took a deep breath as she entered her classroom, her heart still heavy from the frustrations of the previous day. The disrespect and constant challenges from her students had left her feeling defeated, but she refused to give up.

As the students filed in, Aditi noticed Omer in the corner, his gaze fixed on his phone. She knew she had to try a different approach if she wanted to reach him and the rest of the class.

"Good morning, everyone," Aditi began, her voice firm yet warm. "I'd like to start today's class with a discussion about something important: respect."

The students looked up, some with confusion, others with a hint of defiance in their eyes. Omer glanced up from his phone, his eyebrows raised.

"Respect is the foundation of any successful classroom," Aditi continued. "It's not just about how you treat me, your teacher, but how you treat each other. Can anyone tell me what respect means to them?"

A few students shifted uncomfortably in their seats, but Omer spoke up, his tone laced with sarcasm. "Respect? You mean, like, not calling you names or throwing mimicking you?"

Aditi took a deep breath, resisting the urge to react defensively. "Yes, Omer, that's exactly what I mean. Respect is about more than just avoiding disruptive behaviour. It's about understanding each other's perspectives and creating a safe, collaborative environment for learning."

To Aditi's surprise, Omer's expression softened slightly. "I guess that makes sense. My parents are always on my case about 'respecting my elders' and stuff, but they never really explain what that means."

Seizing the opportunity, Aditi nodded. "That's a great point, Omer. Respect isn't just a one-way street. It's about mutual understanding and consideration. Why don't we take a few minutes and have everyone share their thoughts on what respect means to them?"

The class discussion that followed was a revelation for Aditi. As the students opened up, she began to understand the underlying issues they faced – the pressure from their parents, the desire to fit in, and the challenges of navigating a diverse school environment.

Omer, in particular, surprised Aditi with his candid sharing. He spoke about the high expectations his wealthy parents had for him, and how he often felt suffocated by their demands. Aditi listened intently, her heart aching for the young man who seemed to be struggling with his own identity.

"My parents want me to be this perfect student, you know?" Omer said, his voice laced with frustration. "They don't care about what I want. They just want me to get good grades and make them look good."

Aditi nodded empathetically. "I can understand how that must feel, Omer. It's not easy to balance your own needs with the expectations of your family."

The other students in the class began to nod in agreement, sharing their own stories of feeling misunderstood or overlooked by their parents. Aditi realized that by creating a safe space for open discussion, she had unlocked a deeper understanding of her students' lives and the challenges they faced.

As the class discussion drew to a close, Aditi felt a renewed sense of purpose. "Thank you all for sharing your thoughts and experiences. I know it can be difficult to find the right balance between respecting your elders and staying true to yourself. But I believe that if we work together, we can create a classroom environment where everyone feels heard and respected."

Omer met Aditi's gaze, and for the first time, she saw a glimmer of understanding in his eyes. The class erupted into a round of applause, and Aditi knew that she had taken a significant step towards earning their respect.

With a newfound sense of hope, Aditi began to implement a peer accountability system, encouraging the students to support one another in maintaining a respectful classroom. She saw the subtle shifts in their behaviour, as they started to hold each other accountable and celebrate small acts of kindness.

As the chapter drew to a close, Aditi felt a glimmer of hope. She knew the road ahead would still be challenging, but she was determined to continue her fight for respect in the classroom, one student at a time.

The morning sun streamed through the classroom windows, casting a warm glow over the tense atmosphere that had settled in. Aditi Sharma stood at the front of the room; her posture unwavering as she faced a group of disgruntled parents who had come to challenge her teaching methods.

Just moments earlier, Aditi had been forced to reprimand a student for disrupting the class. The incident had escalated quickly, with the student's parents rushing to the school, demanding to speak with the administration. Aditi knew this confrontation was inevitable, but she was determined to stand her ground and advocate for the respect she deserved.

As the parents filed in, Aditi could feel their disapproving glares burning into her. Omer's parents, a wealthy local couple, were at the forefront, their expressions a mix of entitlement and indignation.

"This is unacceptable!" Omer's father exclaimed, slamming his hand on the desk. "My son is being treated unfairly by this...this foreigner!"

Aditi took a deep breath, her eyes meeting that of the man with a steely resolve. "Mr. Patel, I understand your concern, but I must insist that respect and discipline are essential in this classroom. Your son's behaviour was disruptive and disrespectful, and I had no choice but to address it."

The other parents murmured in agreement, some nodding their heads emphatically. Aditi could sense the administration's discomfort, the school administrator shifting nervously in the corner.

"Mrs. Sharma, we understand your position, but you must understand that our children are the priority here," the administrator interjected, his voice laced with a hint of condescension. "Perhaps a more lenient approach would be better received."

Aditi's eyes narrowed; her jaw set with determination. "With all due respect, sir, a 'lenient approach' is exactly what has allowed disrespect to fester in this school. I'm here to educate, not to coddle. My methods may be unconventional, but they are effective in fostering a culture of responsibility and mutual understanding."

The parents exchanged glances, some appearing unsure, while others remained steadfast in their opposition. Omer, who had been sitting quietly in the corner, suddenly stood up, his expression uncharacteristically serious.

"My parents are right, Ms. Aditi. I was out of line earlier, and I should have shown you more respect." He turned to face the other students, his voice carrying a newfound authority. "All of us should be more considerate of our teacher's efforts. She's trying to help us, and we've been taking that for granted."

The room fell silent, the parents and the administrator staring at Omer in stunned disbelief. Aditi felt a surge of pride and hope, her heart swelling with the realization that her efforts were starting to bear fruit.

"Omer is right," she said, addressing the group. "I'm not here to make your lives difficult, but to prepare you for the challenges you'll face in the real world. Respect, discipline, and responsibility are the foundations of success. I know it's not always easy, but I believe in each and every one of you."

Slowly, the parents began to nod, their expressions softening as they recognized the sincerity in Aditi's words. The administrator cleared his throat, his gaze shifting from Aditi to the parents.

"Perhaps we've been too quick to dismiss Ms, Aditi's approach. If the students are willing to cooperate, I believe we should give her methods a chance."

Aditi felt a wave of relief wash over her. This was the breakthrough she had been hoping for, a chance to prove the value of her teaching and to earn the respect she deserved. As the parents filed out, Omer lingered behind, his eyes meeting Aditi's with a newfound sense of understanding.

"I'm sorry, Mrs. Sharma. I'll do better, I promise," he said, his voice soft and sincere.

Aditi smiled, placing a hand on his shoulder. "I know you will, Omer. We're in this together."

With a renewed sense of purpose, Aditi turned her attention to the rest of the class, ready to continue her mission of instilling respect and responsibility in her students. The road ahead might still be challenging, but she was no longer alone in her fight.

CHAPTER SEVENTEEN

BEHIND THE LAUGHTER

The bright spotlights illuminated the stage, casting a warm glow over the packed comedy club. Max, the headliner for the evening, strode up to the microphone, a mischievous grin plastered across his face. The audience erupted in cheers and applause, eager to witness the charismatic comedian's signature brand of humour.

"Good evening, ladies and gentlemen!" Max exclaimed, his voice brimming with energy. "It's so great to see all of your smiling faces tonight. I hope you're ready to laugh your butts off, because that's exactly what I'm here to do!"

The crowd responded with enthusiastic laughter, feeding off Max's infectious energy. He launched into a rapid-fire series of jokes, poking fun at everything from current events to his own quirky idiosyncrasies. His quick wit and self-deprecating charm had the audience in the palm of his hand, their laughter echoing through the dimly lit club.

As the set progressed, Max's performance became more polished and refined, his comedic timing honed to perfection through years of practice. He effortlessly navigated the stage, his lanky frame moving with a natural grace that belied the underlying tension he felt.

Beneath the veneer of his jovial persona, Max's mind was a whirlwind of conflicting emotions. The laughter that filled the room did little to alleviate the deep-seated feelings of inadequacy and depression that had plagued him for as long as he could remember. He had long ago perfected the art of hiding his true self behind a mask of humour, using his comedic talents as a shield against the harsh realities of his life.

Growing up in a household plagued by poverty and family dysfunction, Max had learned at a young age that laughter was the best defence against the pain and uncertainty that surrounded him. His natural talent for comedy had become a means of survival, a way to deflect attention from the emotional turmoil that simmered beneath the surface.

As the final punchline of his set landed, the audience erupted in thunderous applause, their faces alight with joy and amusement. Max basked in the adulation, his smile widening as he acknowledged the crowd's enthusiasm. Yet, the moment the laughter subsided, a familiar emptiness crept back into his heart, a constant reminder that his success on stage did little to fill the void within.

Backstage, Max's demeanour shifted dramatically. The vibrant, energetic persona he had projected onstage melted away, replaced by a weary, introspective figure. He slumped down on a worn couch, his head cradled in his hands as he tried to process the complex emotions swirling through him.

"Another successful set," he muttered to himself, his voice tinged with a hint of bitterness. "So why do I still feel so damn empty?"

Max had long ago mastered the art of making others laugh, but the one thing he struggled to do was to make himself feel genuinely happy. The applause and accolades he received were a temporary balm, a fleeting high that quickly faded, leaving him feeling more isolated and disconnected than ever before.

As he sat in the dimly lit backstage area, Max's mind drifted to the memories of his childhood – the endless nights spent huddled in a cramped apartment, the constant fear of not knowing where the next meal would come from, and the emotional scars left by his parents' tumultuous relationship. These formative experiences had shaped him, moulding him into the jester who now entertained crowds, hiding his pain behind a mask of laughter.

Max's thoughts were interrupted by the sound of his friend Jake's voice, the younger man's brow furrowed with concern.

"Hey, man, you alright?" Jake asked, placing a hand on Max's shoulder. "That was one hell of a set out there. The crowd was eating it up!"

Max forced a smile, his eyes betraying the turmoil that lay beneath the surface. "Yeah, I'm good, Jake. Just a little worn out, that's all."

Jake studied Max's expression, his own face reflecting a growing unease. "You know, you've been killing it on stage lately, but sometimes I can't help but feel like there's something more going on with you. You sure you don't want to talk about it?"

Max hesitated, his instinct to deflect and dismiss his friend's concern warring with a deep-seated desire to open up. For a fleeting moment, he considered confiding in Jake, but the fear of vulnerability and the weight of his own self-imposed isolation ultimately won out.

"Nah, don't worry about it, buddy," Max replied, forcing a chuckle. "I'm just the same old Max, always keeping the laughs coming. That's what I do best, right?"

Jake's expression remained unconvinced, but he knew better than to push the issue further. With a resigned sigh, he gave Max's shoulder a gentle squeeze and headed back out to the main club, leaving the comedian alone with his thoughts.

As the distant sound of laughter and conversation filtered in from the other side of the curtain, Max stared blankly into the shadows, the weight of his own inner turmoil pressing down on him. He had spent so many years perfecting the art of making others laugh, but in the end, it was his own happiness that remained elusive, buried beneath layers of self-doubt and the constant need to hide his true self from the world.

With a heavy heart, Max rose from the couch, his steps slow and deliberate as he made his way out of the club and into the cool night air. The journey ahead would be a difficult one, but as he walked, a glimmer of hope began to flicker within him, a small but persistent flame that promised the possibility of change.

Max sat in the dimly lit auditorium, his fingers drumming nervously on the armrest. He had reluctantly agreed to attend Dr. Elaine's motivational talk, but as the room filled with eager attendees, he felt increasingly out of place. The weight of his own struggles pressed down on him, and he longed for the familiar comfort of the comedy club stage, where he could hide behind the mask of laughter.

As the lights dimmed, Dr. Elaine strode onto the stage, her presence commanding the attention of the audience. Max felt a pang of curiosity, wondering what insights this woman could offer that might resonate with his own inner turmoil.

Dr. Elaine began by sharing her personal story, her voice calm and assured. She spoke of the crippling depression that had once consumed her, the feelings of worthlessness and despair that had threatened to swallow her whole. Max listened, his heart pounding, as she recounted the pivotal moment when she had decided to confront her demons and embark on a journey of self-discovery.

"I had to make a choice," Dr. Elaine said, her gaze sweeping across the audience. "I could continue to hide behind the mask of success, or I could face the darkness head-on and find the light within." Max felt a shiver run down his spine, her words striking a deep chord within him.

As Dr. Elaine shared the steps she had taken to heal, Max found himself leaning forward, his eyes fixed on the stage. She spoke of the importance of vulnerability, of embracing one's flaws and finding strength in the very things that had once seemed like weaknesses. Max's mind raced, his own experiences mirroring the challenges she had faced.

When the talk ended, Max remained seated, lost in thought. The auditorium slowly emptied, but he sat there, unable to move. He had come to this event with the intention of simply going through the motions, of maintaining his carefully constructed facade. But now, something had shifted within him, a glimmer of hope igniting a spark of courage.

Gathering his courage, Max approached the stage, where Dr. Elaine was packing up her notes. She looked up, a warm smile spreading across her face.

"Dr. Elaine," Max began, his voice trembling slightly. "Your story, it... it really resonated with me. I've been struggling with my own demons for so long, and I—" He paused, swallowing hard. "I think I need help."

Dr. Elaine's expression softened, and she placed a reassuring hand on Max's arm. "I'm glad you're here," she said, her voice gentle. "Taking the first step is often the hardest, but it's the most important one."

Max felt a weight lift from his shoulders, as if he had finally given himself permission to be vulnerable. "I don't know where to start," he admitted, his eyes searching hers for guidance.

"That's where I come in," Dr. Elaine replied, her tone reassuring. "Why don't we schedule an appointment, and we can begin this journey together?"

Max nodded, a glimmer of hope flickering in his eyes. "I'd like that," he said, his voice barely above a whisper.

As they made arrangements for their first session, Max felt a sense of trepidation, but also a newfound determination. This was a turning point, a chance to confront the darkness that had been consuming him for so long. He knew the road ahead would not be easy, but for the first time in years, he felt a spark of courage ignite within him.

With a deep breath, Max stepped out into the bustling city streets, his mind already racing with the possibilities that lay ahead. The weight of his past still pressed down on him, but the promise of a brighter future had taken root, and he was ready to begin the journey of self-discovery.

Max sat in Dr. Elaine's cozy office, his fingers nervously tapping the armrest of the plush chair. The walls were adorned with inspirational quotes and certificates, a stark contrast to the turmoil swirling within him. He had taken the first step, mustering the courage to seek help, but the path ahead felt daunting.

“Welcome, Max," Dr. Elaine greeted him with a warm smile, her calm demeanour instantly putting him at ease. "I’m glad you’re here. Why don’t you tell me a bit about what’s been going on?"

Max took a deep breath, his fingers stilling as he met her gaze. "I... I don’t even know where to start," he admitted, his voice laced with a hint of vulnerability. "I’ve been putting on this mask for so long, pretending to be this carefree, funny guy, when inside, I‘m just... lost."

Dr. Elaine nodded empathetically. "It’s understandable to feel that way. Hiding behind a persona can be exhausting. But you’ve taken the first step, and that’s commendable. Now, let’s explore what’s been weighing on you."

As the session progressed, Max found himself opening up in ways he never had before. He shared the details of his childhood, the poverty and family dysfunction that had shaped him. The memories were painful, but there was a sense of relief in finally voicing them.

"My parents were always working, trying to make ends meet," Max explained, his gaze distant. "And when they were home, it was... well, it wasn’t exactly a happy household. There was a lot of tension, a lot of yelling." He paused, swallowing hard. "I guess that’s why I turned to comedy – it was my way of escaping the pain, of making everyone else laugh so they wouldn’t see how broken I felt inside."

Dr. Elaine listened intently, her eyes reflecting a deep understanding. "It’s clear that your upbringing has had a profound impact on you. The need to hide behind a mask, to use laughter as a defence mechanism – these are common coping strategies for those who have experienced trauma and adversity."

Max nodded, feeling a weight lift from his shoulders as he continued to unpack his experiences. He spoke about the societal pressures he faced, the constant need to be "on" and entertaining, and the emptiness he felt after each successful performance.

"I'm good at making people laugh, but it's hollow, you know?" he confessed, his voice laced with frustration. "No matter how much they applaud, no matter how many accolades I receive, I still feel like I'm not enough. Like I'm just a facade, a jester without a heart."

Dr. Elaine leaned forward; her expression compassionate. "That's a heavy burden to carry, Max. But you're here now, taking the first steps towards healing. It's not going to be easy, but I believe you have the strength within you to confront these demons and find true self-acceptance."

As the session drew to a close, Max felt a glimmer of hope ignite within him. He knew the journey ahead would be challenging, but the mere act of opening up had already started to lift the weight from his shoulders.

"Thank you, Dr. Elaine," he said, his voice steadier than it had been at the start of their conversation. "I... I think I'm ready to do the work. To really face myself, no more masks."

Dr. Elaine smiled, her eyes crinkling at the corners. "I'm proud of you, Max. This is the beginning of a transformative process, and I'll be here to guide you every step of the way."

As Max left the office, he felt a renewed sense of determination. The journey within was just beginning, but he was no longer alone. With Dr. Elaine's support and his own newfound courage, he was ready to confront the demons that had haunted him for so long.

In the days that followed, Max's sessions with Dr. Elaine became a sanctuary, a safe space where he could shed his comedic persona and delve into the depths of his psyche. Together, they explored the root causes of his depression, the societal pressures that had shaped his self-perception, and the family dynamics that had left deep scars.

As Max peeled back the layers of his past, he began to uncover the true essence of who he was – a sensitive, intelligent man who had used humor as a shield against the pain of his childhood. With each session, he grew more comfortable in his own skin, learning to embrace the vulnerability he had once feared.

One day, during a particularly poignant session, Max spoke of his estranged relationship with his sister, Lila. "We used to be so close; you know?" he said, his voice tinged with regret. "But after everything that happened with our family, we just... drifted apart. I miss her, but I'm scared to reach out. What if she doesn't want anything to do with me?"

Dr. Elaine listened intently; her eyes filled with empathy. "Reconnecting with Lila could be an important step in your healing journey, Max. Mending that relationship may not be easy, but it could be transformative – for both of you."

Max nodded; his brow furrowed in contemplation. "You're right. I need to at least try. I can't keep running from my past, from the people who matter most to me."

With Dr. Elaine's encouragement, Max mustered the courage to reach out to Lila. The initial conversation was tentative, filled with unspoken emotions and lingering resentments, but slowly, a glimmer of understanding began to emerge. Lila, too, had been grappling with the weight of their shared family history, and the opportunity to reconnect ignited a spark of hope within them both.

As Max's sessions with Dr. Elaine continued, he found himself embracing self-love in ways he had never imagined. The process was not without its challenges, but with each breakthrough, he felt a little lighter, a little more whole. The mask he had worn for so long was gradually peeling away, revealing the authentic Max – flawed, vulnerable, and ultimately, resilient.

With a renewed sense of purpose, Max began to explore the possibility of incorporating his journey into his comedy. The idea both excited and terrified him, but he knew that if he wanted to truly connect with his audience, he had to be willing to share his truth.

As he stood on the brink of a significant performance, Max felt a surge of determination. This time, he would not hide behind the mask of the jester. Instead, he would embrace the power of his own story, using his platform to inspire and uplift others who might be struggling with their own demons.

The journey within had been arduous, but Max was ready to take the stage and show the world the real him – scars and all.

The auditorium was abuzz with anticipation as the crowd eagerly awaited Max's performance. He stood backstage, his heart pounding in his chest, the weight of his decision to share his authentic story weighing heavily on his mind.

For years, Max had hidden behind the mask of a jester, using his quick wit and sarcastic humour to shield himself from the pain and vulnerability that lurked beneath the surface. But now, after his sessions with Dr. Elaine, he knew that the time had come to shed that facade and embrace his true self.

As he took a deep breath, the memories of his journey flooded his mind. The empty feeling that had haunted him after his successful comedy sets, the transformative experience of attending Dr. Elaine's talk, and the difficult yet necessary exploration of his past – all of it had led him to this moment.

Max stepped out onto the stage, his eyes scanning the sea of faces before him. The audience, initially buzzing with excitement, fell silent as they sensed the shift in his demeanour. Gone was the confident, larger-than-life persona they had come to expect; in its place stood a man who radiated a raw, honest vulnerability.

"Good evening, everyone," Max began, his voice soft and tentative. "I, uh, I want to thank you all for being here tonight. I know you're probably expecting the same old song and dance from me – the quick-witted jokester who makes you laugh until your sides hurt." He paused, a wistful smile playing on his lips. "But tonight, I want to do something a little different."

The audience shifted in their seats, unsure of what to expect. Max took another deep breath and continued, "You see, for a long time, I've been hiding behind a mask – a mask of laughter and humour that I've used to shield myself from the pain and struggles that I've been facing." He paused, his gaze sweeping across the crowd. "Depression, feelings of inadequacy, a troubled past – these are the demons that I've been battling, and for years, I've used comedy as a way to escape them."

A hush fell over the audience as Max's words sank in. Some nodded in understanding, while others leaned forward, captivated by his raw honesty.

"But tonight, I'm ready to take off that mask," Max said, his voice gaining strength. "I'm ready to share my authentic self with all of you – the good, the bad, and the ugly. Because I've learned that true healing and self-acceptance can only come when we're willing to be vulnerable and embrace our flaws."

As he spoke, Max could feel the walls he had built around himself slowly crumbling. The weight of his past, the burden of his depression, and the fear of rejection – all of it was being laid bare for the world to see. But in that moment, he felt a sense of liberation, a freedom that he had never experienced before.

"Growing up, I faced a lot of challenges – poverty, family trauma, and the constant pressure to be someone I wasn't," Max continued, his gaze darkening as he recalled those difficult memories. "Comedy became my way of coping, my way of hiding from the pain. But it was never a true solution. It was just a mask, a facade that I hid behind, afraid to confront the truth of who I really was."

The audience listened in rapt silence, the only sound the occasional sniffle or soft murmur of empathy.

"It wasn't until I met Dr. Elaine that I started to understand the importance of self-acceptance and the power of vulnerability," Max said, a glimmer of hope in his eyes. "She helped me to see that my struggles, my flaws, and my pain – they're all a part of what makes me who I am. And that's something to be embraced, not hidden away."

He paused, his gaze sweeping across the audience once more. "So tonight, I'm not here to make you laugh. I'm here to share my story, to connect with you on a deeper level, and to hopefully inspire you to embrace your own authentic selves – with all of your imperfections and struggles."

As Max's words echoed through the auditorium, the audience erupted in a thunderous applause, their cheers and shouts of support filling the air. Some wiped tears from their eyes, while others nodded in understanding, their own experiences mirroring the journey that Max had described.

In that moment, Max felt a weight lift from his shoulders. The mask he had worn for so long had been cast aside, and in its place stood a man who was finally comfortable in his own skin – a man who had found the courage to share his truth with the world.

As the applause died down, Max stepped forward, a small, genuine smile playing on his lips. "Thank you all for being here tonight," he said, his voice steady and sincere. "Let's continue this journey together, shall we?"

The audience erupted in cheers once more, their enthusiasm and support fuelling Max's newfound sense of purpose. He knew that the road ahead would not be easy, but with the courage he had found and the support of those around him, he was ready to embrace his authentic self and inspire others to do the same.

As he stepped off the stage, Max felt a sense of pride and relief wash over him. The performance had been a cathartic release, a moment of vulnerability that had resonated with the audience in a way he had never anticipated. And as he caught sight of his sister, Lila, in the crowd, her eyes shining with tears of pride, he knew that this was just the beginning of a new chapter in his life – one filled with self-acceptance, healing, and the power of authentic connection.

CHAPTER EIGHTEEN

BETWEEN TRADITION AND FUTURE

The sterile white walls of the clinic seemed to close in around Maya as she stared at the ultrasound image. Her fingers traced the delicate outline of the tiny life growing within her, a mixture of wonder and trepidation washing over her. The doctor's words echoed in her ears—"Congratulations, you're approximately eight weeks pregnant"—but all she could hear was the thundering of her own heartbeat.

Outside, Mumbai's chaotic streets hummed with their usual energy, a stark contrast to the quiet intensity of Maya's internal world. At twenty-eight, she had always been the responsible one in her family, the daughter who balanced tradition with modern aspirations. This pregnancy was both a blessing and a challenge she hadn't fully anticipated.

When she arrived home, the apartment was dark except for the flickering blue light of the television. Vaishnav sat hunched over his gaming console, headset on, completely absorbed in his virtual world. Maya watched him for a moment, her excitement deflating like a punctured balloon.

"Vaishnav," she said softly, then louder, "Vaishnav!"

He raised a hand without turning, a gesture that was simultaneously a acknowledgment and a dismissal. "Just a sec, babe. I'm in the middle of a crucial mission."

Maya felt a familiar frustration rising. She walked closer, deliberately standing between Vaishnav and the television. "I need to talk to you about something important."

Vaishnav's character on screen died, and he let out an exasperated sigh. He pushed his headset back, revealing a face that was more irritated than interested. "What's so urgent?"

Taking a deep breath, Maya said the words she had rehearsed in her mind countless times during the clinic visit. "I'm pregnant."

Silence hung between them. Vaishnav blinked, then turned back to reset his game. "That's nice," he mumbled, his attention already drifting back to the screen.

"Nice?" Maya's voice rose, a mix of disbelief and anger. "We're having a child, and all you can say is 'nice'?"

Before Vaishnav could respond—or more likely, ignore her—the apartment buzzer rang. Sruthi, Vaishnav's sister, didn't wait for an invitation. She swept in with her usual dramatic flair, her designer handbag swinging dramatically.

"Well, well," Sruthi said, her eyes scanning Maya with a critical gaze. "You look... different."

Maya knew that look. It was the same calculating expression Sruthi always wore when she was about to deliver a passive-aggressive comment. "I'm pregnant," Maya stated firmly, deciding to take control of the narrative.

Sruthi's perfectly manicured eyebrow arched. "Pregnant? How... unexpected." The way she said it made the word sound like an accusation.

That evening, during a family dinner at Vaishnav's parents' upscale apartment, the real drama unfolded. Deepak, Vaishnav's father, listened to the pregnancy announcement with a calculating expression that reminded Maya of a banker assessing a risky investment.

"A child?" Anjali, Vaishnav's mother, said, her voice tight. "Have you considered the financial implications?"

Maya watched Vaishnav, hoping for support. But he remained silent, pushing food around his plate, avoiding eye contact with everyone.

"We've calculated the expenses," Deepak said, pulling out a spreadsheet. "Medical costs, education, potential career interruptions for Maya. It's not a small matter."

The subtext was clear: the baby was more of a financial burden than a blessing.

Maya felt a surge of determination. She might be pregnant, but she wasn't helpless. "I'll continue working," she said firmly. "I'm taking online courses, and I've been exploring freelance opportunities."

Sruthi's laugh was sharp. "Freelance? With a baby?"

But Maya had stopped listening. She looked at Vaishnav, who was still avoiding her gaze, and realized the journey ahead would require her strength, her resilience.

As the evening concluded, Maya understood that this pregnancy was more than just bringing a child into the world. It was about proving her worth, her capability, her independence.

The baby growing inside her was already teaching her something profound: sometimes, the most significant battles are fought not with others, but within oneself.

The morning sunlight filtered through the curtains of Maya and Vaishnav's modest apartment, casting a soft glow on the scattered gaming controllers and half-empty coffee mugs. Maya sat at the kitchen table, her laptop open, fingers hovering over the keyboard as she scrolled through job listings. The pregnancy test tucked away in her drawer felt like a silent reminder of the challenges ahead.

Sruthi's voice echoed in her mind from their recent encounter. "A baby? Right now? With Vaishnav's gaming addiction and your uncertain career?" The words were carefully chosen, designed to cut deep and plant seeds of doubt.

Maya took a deep breath, pushing away the negativity. She clicked on a freelance writing position, her determination rising with each job description. If Vaishnav wouldn't step up, she would secure their future herself.

The sound of Vaishnav's gaming filled the background—loud explosions and competitive shouts punctuating the tense silence between them. Maya turned, watching her husband completely absorbed in his virtual world, oblivious to the real-world challenges mounting around them.

"Vaishnav," she called, her voice steady but firm. No response.

She walked closer, standing directly behind him. "Vaishnav, we need to talk about our financial situation."

He raised a hand, dismissively waving her away. "Not now, Maya. I'm in the middle of a crucial match."

The dismissal ignited a spark of frustration within her. Maya reached over and switched off the gaming console, causing Vaishnav to spin around, his face a mixture of shock and anger.

"What the hell?" he protested.

"We're having a baby," Maya stated, her voice calm but resolute. "And right now, we're not prepared. Your parents have made it clear they're worried about financial implications, and you've been doing nothing but playing games."

Vaishnav's defensive mechanism kicked in immediately. "My parents are always worried about something. They're professional worriers."

"They're not entirely wrong this time," Maya countered. "We need a plan. I've been looking at freelance opportunities, but I'll need your support."

A tense silence hung between them. Vaishnav avoided her gaze, his fingers nervously tapping against his leg. Maya noticed something else—a slight bulge in his jacket pocket that looked suspiciously like an envelope.

"What's that?" she asked, pointing.

Vaishnav's hand instinctively moved to cover the pocket. "Nothing."

But Maya knew better. She stepped forward, her maternal instinct and growing independence giving her courage. "Show me."

Reluctantly, Vaishnav pulled out an envelope. Bank statements spilled out, revealing a savings account Maya knew nothing about. Her heart raced—not from anger, but from the realization of how disconnected they had become.

"You've been hiding money?" she asked, her voice a mix of hurt and determination.

"It's just... my gaming tournament winnings," Vaishnav mumbled. "I was going to tell you."

But they both knew that was a lie.

Outside their apartment, the urban neighbourhood hummed with life—a stark contrast to the tension building inside. Families walked by, children laughing, a reminder of the future that was growing inside Maya.

Sruthi's words from earlier returned: "Are you sure Vaishnav is ready to be a father?"

Maya looked at her husband, seeing not the immature gamer, but a man at a crossroads. He could choose growth or continue his current path.

"We're going to need a plan," Maya said softly. "For our child."

Vaishnav remained silent, the weight of impending fatherhood slowly sinking in.

The morning sunlight filtered through the curtains of their small apartment, casting a soft glow on Maya's determined face. She sat at the kitchen table, her laptop open, fingers flying across the keyboard as she explored online freelance writing opportunities. Each click represented more than just a potential job—it was a step towards financial independence and security for her unborn child.

Her phone buzzed. Another message from her sister-in-law Sruthi. Maya's jaw tightened as she read the passive-aggressive text: "Heard you're looking for work. Are you sure you can handle a job and a pregnancy? Maybe you should focus on being a good wife instead."

Maya took a deep breath, refusing to let Sruthi's manipulation affect her. She knew the real motivation behind these messages—Sruthi's desperate attempt to maintain her status as the centre of attention in the family. With calculated precision, Maya drafted a professional response that was both polite and firm, then returned to her job search.

Later that afternoon, the tension escalated when Deepak and Anjali arrived unannounced. Their faces were masks of disapproval, their body language radiating disappointment. Vaishnav sat uncomfortably on the edge of the sofa, avoiding eye contact.

"We need to discuss the situation," Deepak began, his voice carrying the weight of patriarchal authority. "This pregnancy is ill-timed. Your financial instability is concerning."

Maya stood her ground, her voice steady and controlled. "With all due respect, this is our child. We will manage our finances and our future."

Anjali interjected, her tone dripping with condescension. "Manage? Look at your current situation. Vaishnav barely earns enough, and now you want to work? Who will take care of the child?"

The implication was clear—they wanted Maya to consider alternatives. The unspoken suggestion of termination hung in the air like a toxic cloud.

Vaishnav remained silent, a characteristic that infuriated Maya. His continued passivity in the face of his parents' manipulation was becoming unbearable.

"I will work," Maya declared, her voice rising with conviction. "I will ensure our child has everything they need. My career doesn't end with pregnancy—it continues."

Sruthi, who had been lurking in the background, chose this moment to add her toxic commentary. "Are you sure you can handle both? Most women struggle. Maybe you're not cut out for this."

The calculated words were designed to undermine Maya's confidence, but they had the opposite effect. Each attempt to break her only made her more resolute.

As the confrontation reached its peak, Maya experienced a sudden moment of physical discomfort—a sharp pain that made her momentarily clutch her stomach. The room fell silent.

Vaishnav, finally jolted from his passive state, rushed to her side. "Maya? Are you okay?"

The health scare was brief but significant. It forced Vaishnav to confront the reality of impending fatherhood and the potential consequences of his family's toxic behaviour. For the first time, a flicker of understanding crossed his face.

The in-laws exchanged worried glances. The possibility of something happening to the pregnancy—their potential grandchild—suddenly made the situation feel more real.

Maya's resilience shone through. Even in moments of physical vulnerability, her mental strength remained unbroken. "I'm fine," she said firmly. "But this conversation is over."

Her declaration was met with stunned silence. Deepak, Anjali, and Sruthi realized they were facing a woman who would not be intimidated or controlled.

As they left, the dynamics had subtly shifted. Vaishnav looked at Maya with a newfound respect, a hint of admiration replacing his previous indifference.

Maya knew the battle was far from over. But today, she had drawn a line in the sand. Her child would be born into a world where their mother's strength was unquestionable, where family expectations would not dictate her worth or potential.

The breaking point had become her moment of triumph.

The sterile white walls of the hospital delivery room seemed to pulse with anticipation. Maya's breaths came in sharp, measured gasps, her body trembling with each contraction. Vaishnav stood beside her, his hand surprisingly steady as he gripped hers—a stark contrast to his previous detached demeanour.

"You're doing amazing," he whispered, his voice breaking slightly. The past weeks of tension—the arguments, the gaming, the family pressures—seemed to dissolve in this singular moment of vulnerability.

Dr. Sharma's calm voice cut through the room. "One more push, Maya. You're almost there."

Maya's grip on Vaishnav's hand tightened, her determination etched across her face. This was more than just giving birth—this was her moment of triumph, of proving her strength to everyone who had doubted her.

A piercing cry filled the room. Their son.

As the nurse cleaned the newborn, Vaishnav found himself transfixed. The tiny human before him was nothing like the digital characters he'd spent countless hours manipulating in his video games. This was real. This was life.

"Would you like to cut the umbilical cord?" the nurse asked Vaishnav.

For a moment, he hesitated—a reflection of his past self. But something had shifted. Without a word, he stepped forward, his hands surprisingly gentle as he completed the symbolic act of separation and connection.

Outside the delivery room, a different drama was unfolding. Sruthi paced the corridor, her carefully constructed facade of indifference cracking. Deepak and Anjali sat in uncomfortable silence, the weight of their manipulations hanging heavily between them.

"This changes everything," Anjali muttered, more to herself than to anyone else.

Sruthi's sharp laugh cut through the tension. "Does it, though?"

But even she knew something fundamental had changed. Maya's unwavering strength during her pregnancy, her refusal to be manipulated, had fundamentally altered the family's dynamics.

Back in the room, Maya cradled her son. Her eyes met Vaishnav's, a silent communication passing between them. The journey hadn't been easy—the arguments, the financial pressures, Sruthi's constant undermining—but they had arrived at this moment.

"I'm sorry," Vaishnav said softly, the words carrying the weight of his past indifference. "For everything."

Maya didn't immediately respond. Her silence was deliberate, a boundary she was establishing. This wasn't about instant forgiveness, but about genuine transformation.

As if sensing the emotional complexity, the baby stirred, his tiny hand reaching out and inadvertently touching both his parents—a symbolic gesture of connection and hope.

Later that evening, as the hospital room settled into a quiet rhythm, Vaishnav made a decision that would surprise everyone. He pulled out his gaming console—the object that had been a source of so much conflict—and placed it in the hospital trash bin.

"I'm done," he said simply to Maya. "This isn't who I want to be anymore."

The gesture was more than just discarding a gaming system. It was a commitment—to his wife, to his child, to himself.

Outside, Deepak approached the nurse's station, his usual authoritative demeanour slightly subdued. "How is my daughter-in-law?" he asked, a hint of genuine concern replacing his typical transactional approach.

The nurse, sensing the complexity of the family dynamics, offered a professional smile. "Mother and child are doing well."

Sruthi watched from a distance, her manipulative strategies suddenly feeling hollow. The baby's arrival had exposed the fragility of her attempts to control the family narrative.

As night fell, the hospital room became a microcosm of transformation. Maya, exhausted but triumphant, held her sleeping son. Vaishnav sat nearby, no longer distracted, but present—truly present.

The baby represented more than just a new life. He was a symbol of resilience, of hope, of the possibility of change. In his first hours of life, he had already begun to reshape the intricate dynamics of a family teetering between tradition and modernity.

Outside, the urban landscape of Mumbai continued its relentless rhythm—a perfect metaphor for the continuous, challenging, yet beautiful journey of family that was unfolding within these hospital walls.

CHAPTER NINETEEN

THE HIDDEN WOUNDS

The fluorescent lights of Synergy Solutions cast a harsh glare across the open-plan office, illuminating Gauri's meticulously organized workspace. Her fingers moved with practiced precision across the keyboard, each keystroke a testament to her professional excellence. To her colleagues, she was the epitome of corporate perfection—sharp blazer, immaculate hair, a smile that never quite reached her eyes.

Gauri glanced up, catching the concerned look of her team lead. She adjusted her posture, smoothing an invisible wrinkle from her sleeve. Years of conditioning had taught her to maintain a flawless exterior, to hide the turmoil brewing beneath the surface.

As the morning progressed, Gauri's movements became slightly more measured. A subtle discomfort flickered across her face—quickly masked by a professional smile when a colleague approached her desk. "Everything okay, Gauri?" asked Rahul, her project coordinator.

"Perfectly fine," she responded, her voice crisp and controlled. "Just working on the quarterly report."

But everything was not fine. The previous night's encounter with her husband had left more than just emotional scars. The memory of his aggressive behaviour, the complete disregard for her well-being, burned in her mind. She remembered the rough intimacy, his complete lack of concern for her health, the growing sense of violation that had become her daily reality.

Across the office, Athulya moved with a different energy. Her charm was effortless, her wit sharp enough to cut through the monotonous corporate atmosphere. To anyone watching, she appeared confident, engaging in conversations with colleagues, her laughter a carefully crafted melody of social performance.

Yet behind her sparkling eyes lay a different story. Her marriage was a delicate construct, a facade carefully maintained to meet societal expectations. Married to a gay man who was equally trapped by familial and social pressures, Athulya understood the art of performance better than most.

During the mid-morning coffee break, Athulya found herself near Gauri. Their proximity was coincidental, but something unspoken passed between them—a shared understanding of silent suffering.

"Tough morning?" Athulya asked, her voice low and empathetic.

Gauri hesitated, then offered a controlled smile. "Just the usual corporate challenges."

In the corner of the office, partially obscured by a strategically placed plant, Anjali watched. As the company counsellor, she had developed a keen sense for unspoken narratives. Gauri's slight physical discomfort, Athulya's carefully constructed exterior—these were stories she had seen countless times.

Her professional notebook lay open, but she made no immediate notes. Observation was her first tool, discretion her most valued skill.

By afternoon, Gauri could no longer ignore the physical symptoms. A burning sensation, a growing discomfort that spoke of more than just stress. Her professional demeanour began to crack, tiny fissures of vulnerability showing through her meticulously maintained exterior.

She excused herself from a team meeting, her steps measured but slightly unsteady. The office bathroom became her temporary sanctuary, a moment of privacy where the mask could slip, if only for a few moments.

Athulya noticed Gauri's departure. Something in the other woman's movement—a combination of pain and determination—resonated deeply with her own experiences of navigating personal challenges while maintaining a professional front.

As the workday drew to a close, Gauri made a decision. The symptoms she was experiencing could no longer be ignored. Despite the societal stigma, despite the shame that threatened to consume her, she would seek medical help.

Her fingers trembled slightly as she gathered her belongings. The facade was cracking, and behind it, a journey of recovery and self-discovery was about to begin.

Little did Gauri know that her path would soon intersect more deeply with Athulya's, guided by the watchful, compassionate eyes of Anjali—the counsellor who understood that every story of struggle was also a potential story of transformation.

The office lights began to dim, another day of corporate life drawing to a close. But for Gauri, a more significant journey was just beginning—a journey towards understanding her worth, her health, and her right to respect.

Gauri's fingers trembled as she dialled her mother's number. The familiar ring echoed in her ear, each second stretching into an eternity. She had rehearsed this conversation countless times, but now, faced with the reality of it, words seemed to evaporate from her mind.

"Hello, beta?" Her mother's voice, warm and comforting, filled the line.

Gauri took a deep breath. "Maa, I... I need to talk to you about something important."

As Gauri poured out her concerns about her health issues, her mother's initial sympathy quickly morphed into a mixture of shock and disapproval. "But beta, these things happen in marriage. You must adjust," her mother advised, her voice laced with the weight of generational expectations.

Gauri felt a familiar knot forming in her throat. "Maa, it's not just about adjusting. My health is at risk. I need to see a doctor."

The ensuing silence spoke volumes. Gauri could almost see her mother's furrowed brow, the internal struggle between maternal concern and societal norms playing out in her mind. "What will people say?" her mother finally whispered, more to herself than to Gauri.

Across town, in the serene confines of Anjali's office, Athulya sat perched on the edge of a plush armchair, her usual confident demeanour replaced by a vulnerability rarely seen in the workplace.

"I feel like I'm suffocating, Anjali," Athulya confessed, her voice barely above a whisper. "Every day, I put on this mask of the perfect wife, the successful professional. But inside? I'm screaming."

Anjali leaned forward, her eyes reflecting a deep understanding. "Tell me more about this mask, Athulya. What's underneath it?"

Athulya's laugh was hollow. "A woman who married young to please her family, only to realize her husband... well, let's just say we're better off as friends. A woman who dreams of a love she's never known, of a life where she doesn't have to pretend."

As Athulya's session concluded, Gauri found herself in a stark, clinical waiting room. The decision to visit a doctor had been a battle, each step feeling like a betrayal to the facade she had so carefully constructed. But as the nurse called her name, Gauri squared her shoulders. This was more than a medical visit; it was her first step towards reclaiming her life.

The corporate retreat buzzed with energy, a stark contrast to the turmoil in Athulya's mind. As she navigated through networking sessions and team-building exercises, she felt more isolated than ever. It wasn't until a chance encounter with Ravi, a colleague from another department, that Athulya felt a glimmer of hope.

"You know, Athulya," Ravi said, his voice low and sincere, "happiness isn't a luxury. It's a right. And sometimes, we need to fight for it, even if it means going against the grain."

His words echoed in Athulya's mind long after their conversation ended. For the first time in years, she allowed herself to imagine a life beyond the confines of her loveless marriage.

As the day drew to a close, Gauri and Athulya found themselves in their respective spaces, each woman experiencing a profound moment of clarity. Gauri, curled up on her couch, cradled a cup of tea, the doctor's words still ringing in her ears. The diagnosis was clear, the treatment path laid out. But more than that, it was the doctor's compassionate yet firm stance on her right to health and respect that had shaken Gauri to her core.

In her apartment across the city, Athulya stood before her mirror, really seeing herself for the first time in years. She traced the lines of worry that had etched themselves around her eyes, testament to years of silent suffering. But there was something else there too – a spark of defiance, of hope.

Both women, unknown to each other, shared a similar thought: they were not alone. In a society that often prioritized appearances over well-being, in a corporate world that demanded perfection at all costs, their struggles were not isolated incidents. They were part of a larger narrative, one that was begging to be acknowledged and addressed.

As Gauri set down her tea and reached for her phone, determined to research support groups, Athulya picked up a pen and began to write. It started as a journal entry but quickly transformed into a manifesto of sorts – a promise to herself to pursue authenticity and happiness, regardless of the cost.

The chapter of pretence was closing. A new one, fraught with challenges but brimming with possibility, was just beginning. In the quiet of their respective homes, Gauri and Athulya took their first tentative steps towards a future where they could stand tall, unburdened by the weight of societal expectations and personal demons.

Little did they know that their paths, already intertwined in ways they couldn't imagine, were about to converge in a powerful alliance of mutual support and understanding. As the night settled over the city, two women, separated by distance but united in their quest for self-respect and happiness, found themselves at the threshold of transformation.

The fluorescent lights of Synergy Solutions cast a harsh glare across Gauri's pale face. Her body felt like a battlefield—each movement a reminder of the infection that was slowly consuming her physical and emotional strength. The morning meeting dragged on, her mind drifting between professional composure and the mounting tension brewing within her.

During a brief coffee break, Gauri found herself standing next to Athulya. Their earlier encounters had been polite but distant, but today something felt different. A shared understanding flickered between them—a silent acknowledgment of unspoken struggles.

"Are you okay?" Athulya's voice was soft, her eyes carrying a depth of empathy that caught Gauri off guard.

Gauri hesitated, her professional mask momentarily slipping. "I've been better," she admitted, surprising herself with the unexpected vulnerability.

Their conversation was interrupted by a work emergency, but the moment lingered—a connection forged in the quiet spaces between professional expectations and personal pain.

Later that afternoon, Gauri's resolve finally broke. The physical discomfort of her infection, combined with months of her husband's neglect and abuse, pushed her to a critical point. When she returned home, the confrontation was inevitable.

"I'm sick," Gauri stated firmly to her husband, her voice steady despite the trembling inside. "And it's because of your complete disregard for basic hygiene and respect."

The room filled with a tense silence. Her husband's initial dismissive attitude quickly transformed into anger, his voice rising. "What are you talking about? What nonsense are you spreading?"

Gauri stood her ground. Years of suppressed emotions erupted. "I'm talking about the infection I've developed. I'm talking about the constant neglect. I'm talking about the fact that I deserve basic human dignity."

Simultaneously, Athulya was experiencing her own moment of transformation. During a conversation with Anjali, the counselor subtly introduced her to a divorce support group. The mere suggestion felt like a lifeline.

"Sometimes," Anjali explained gently, "recognizing that you deserve happiness is the first step towards creating it."

Athulya's strategic mind began processing the information. Her marriage had been a facade—a construct built to meet societal expectations. The support group represented more than just legal advice; it was a pathway to authenticity.

Back at Synergy Solutions, Anjali began documenting the journeys of Gauri and Athulya. Her notes reflected a deeper understanding of the complex narratives navigated by women—stories of survival, resilience, and reclamation.

"Relationship hygiene isn't just about physical cleanliness," she wrote in her confidential report. "It's about emotional respect, mutual understanding, and the fundamental right to personal dignity."

The chance meeting between Gauri and Athulya later that week became a pivotal moment. During a quiet corner of the office, away from prying eyes, they shared a candid conversation.

"I never thought I'd say this," Gauri confided, "but I'm considering divorce."

Athulya's response was immediate and supportive. "It takes immense courage to choose yourself."

Their conversation wasn't just about their individual struggles—it was about breaking generational patterns of silence and submission. Each word they exchanged was a small act of rebellion against the conservative societal norms that had confined them.

As the day concluded, Gauri made her decision. The medical diagnosis, her husband's continued neglect, and her conversation with Athulya crystallized her resolve. She would seek a divorce. She would prioritize her health. She would reclaim her life.

The chapter ended with a sense of potential—a delicate but powerful momentum towards personal transformation. Gauri and Athulya, once isolated in their struggles, now stood on the precipice of change, their stories intertwined by a shared understanding of resilience.

Anjali watched from a distance, a quiet smile acknowledging the strength of these women who were rewriting their narratives, one difficult conversation at a time.

The sterile white walls of Anjali's counselling office felt different today—less confining and more like a sanctuary of possibility. Gauri sat carefully; her posture rigid but her eyes holding a newfound determination. Her medical treatment had begun, and with it came a slow but steady transformation of her inner landscape.

"How are you feeling about the treatment?" Anjali asked, her voice soft yet professional.

Gauri took a deep breath. "Scared, but also... relieved. For the first time, I'm prioritizing my health." Her fingers traced the edge of her medical report, a tangible symbol of her journey towards self-recovery.

Meanwhile, across the office, Athulya was preparing for her own moment of confrontation. Her husband, Rahul, had agreed to meet her for a conversation that would change everything. The divorce support group Anjali had recommended had given her unexpected courage.

Their text messages had become a lifeline—short, supportive exchanges that bridged their individual struggles.

Gauri: "Today, I'm learning about setting boundaries."

Athulya: "One step at a time. We've got this."

At home, Athulya carefully selected her words. When Rahul arrived, she was calm, almost serene. "We need to talk about our marriage," she began, her strategic mind already mapping out the conversation.

Rahul looked uncomfortable but listened as Athulya explained her understanding of their situation. "We've both been living a lie," she said. "You deserve to be with someone who truly loves you, and so do I."

The conversation was emotional but respectful—a testament to their years of friendship and mutual understanding. They discussed logistics, feelings, and most importantly, their individual paths to authenticity.

At Synergy Solutions, Anjali was preparing a workshop that would become a turning point for many. "Relationship Hygiene and Respect" was more than just a corporate training session—it was a manifesto of empowerment.

Gauri and Athulya sat next to each other during the workshop, their solidarity palpable. Anjali's presentation wasn't just about physical health, but emotional well-being. She spoke about recognizing toxic relationships, understanding consent, and the importance of mutual respect.

"Hygiene isn't just about physical cleanliness," Anjali explained, her eyes scanning the room. "It's about emotional spaces, boundaries, and treating yourself and your partner with dignity."

Gauri felt a surge of recognition. Her journey wasn't just about medical treatment—it was about healing her entire self. Athulya, listening intently, realized her path to happiness required similar courage.

During a break, they shared a moment of connection. "How are you feeling?" Gauri asked Athulya.

Athulya's laugh was genuine, tinged with a newfound lightness. "Terrified and excited. Like I'm finally writing my own story."

Their text support continued, now supplemented by in-person conversations. They were no longer just colleagues navigating similar struggles—they were allies in a journey of self-discovery.

As the workshop concluded, both women felt a profound shift. The conservative corporate environment that had once felt suffocating now seemed like a space of potential transformation.

Anjali watched them, documenting their progress. Each woman's story was unique, yet they shared a common thread of resilience. Their journeys weren't just about ending unhealthy relationships—they were about beginning powerful, authentic lives.

The chapter closed with a sense of hope. Gauri's medical treatment progressed, Athulya prepared for her next conversation with Rahul, and both women understood that their strength lay not in perfection, but in their willingness to heal, grow, and support each other.

Their paths to empowerment were just beginning.

The soft morning light filtered through the café windows, casting a warm glow on Gauri and Athulya's table. Their coffee cups sat half-empty, a testament to the deep conversation that had been unfolding between them. Gauri's fingers traced the rim of her mug, her movements more confident than they had been just weeks ago.

"I never thought I'd be here," Gauri said, a hint of wonder in her voice. "Happy, I mean. Truly happy."

Athulya reached out and squeezed her friend's hand. The journey they had shared was more than just a professional connection—it was a bond forged through mutual understanding and shared struggles. Her own life had transformed dramatically. Gone was the woman who had once lived in fear and conformity, replaced by someone who had discovered the courage to be authentically herself.

"Remember when we first started talking?" Athulya asked, a playful smile dancing on her lips. "We were both wearing these perfect masks, hiding everything that was breaking inside us."

Gauri nodded, her eyes reflecting a mix of pain and triumph. Her recent relationship was nothing like her previous marriage. David, the man she was now dating, understood the meaning of respect in a way her ex-husband never had. He listened, supported her medical treatment, and most importantly, treated her as an equal.

"The treatment was challenging," Gauri shared, her voice steady. "But Anjali's guidance and your support made all the difference. I'm not just healing physically, but emotionally too."

Athulya's own journey had been equally transformative. She had met Aria at the divorce support group—a woman who understood the complexities of finding oneself after years of living a prescribed life. Their relationship was built on mutual respect, understanding, and genuine connection.

"I never imagined I could be this happy," Athulya admitted. "Breaking free from my marriage to Rahul, accepting my true self—it's been liberating."

Their conversation was interrupted by a text from Anjali. The counsellor had been documenting their stories, preparing a presentation on relationship dynamics and personal empowerment. Her work had gained significant attention within the corporate circles, challenging traditional narratives about marriage and personal growth.

As they continued talking, the café around them buzzed with life. But for Gauri and Athulya, the world had shrunk to this moment—a celebration of their resilience, their friendship, and their hard-won independence.

"We're not just survivors," Gauri said, her voice filled with conviction. "We're creators of our own happiness."

Athulya raised her coffee cup in a toast. "To new beginnings," she said.

"To new beginnings," Gauri echoed.

Later that evening, as Gauri prepared for a date with David and Athulya planned a weekend getaway with Aria, they reflected on their journeys. The corporate world that had once felt like a constraint now seemed like a platform for transformation.

Anjali's words from one of her workshops resonated with them: "Relationship hygiene isn't just about physical health. It's about emotional respect, personal boundaries, and the courage to choose yourself."

Their stories were more than personal narratives. They were testimonies to the power of self-discovery, the importance of support, and the incredible strength that emerges when women refuse to be defined by societal expectations.

As the day drew to a close, Gauri and Athulya knew their journeys were far from over. But they were no longer afraid. They were empowered, connected, and most importantly, they were free.

CHAPTER TWENTY

EMBRACING THE UNSEEN

The sterile white walls of Dr. Martinez's office seemed to close in on Sarah as she gripped the edge of her chair. Her fingers, usually steady, trembled slightly against the cold plastic armrest. The paediatrician's words hung in the air, suspended between them like a delicate, fragile thing.

"Down syndrome," Dr. Martinez had said gently, her eyes filled with a compassion that did little to soften the impact of the diagnosis.

Ethan lay peacefully in his carrier, oblivious to the moment that would forever divide Sarah's life into "before" and "after." His tiny fingers curled softly, his round cheeks a perfect contrast to the clinical environment. He was beautiful – impossibly, breathtakingly beautiful. But in that moment, all Sarah could feel was a tsunami of emotions threatening to overwhelm her.

Dreams she had carefully constructed since the moment she knew she was pregnant began to crumble. The vision of soccer games, school plays, college graduations – they now seemed like fragile glass sculptures, threatening to shatter with the slightest touch. Would Ethan be able to do all the things she had imagined? Would the world see him the way she saw him?

Driving home, Sarah's mind raced. The road blurred through tears she refused to let fall. Ethan cooed softly in the backseat, a sound that should have brought comfort but instead felt like a painful reminder of the uncertainty that lay ahead.

At home, the silence was deafening. Mark, her husband, was at work, and Sarah found herself alone with her thoughts and her son. She traced Ethan's features – the slight upward tilt of his eyes, the unique curve of his ears. Medical textbooks and online resources she'd frantically researched played like a continuous loop in her mind. Statistics, potential challenges, medical considerations – they swirled together in a dizzying mix of information and fear.

"I'm sorry," she whispered to Ethan, though she wasn't entirely sure what she was apologizing for. For her fear? For the challenges he might face? For the world that might not understand him?

Days passed, and Sarah's world became smaller. She stopped going to mommy groups, avoided conversations with other parents. The weight of the diagnosis felt like a barrier, separating her from the world she once knew. Each interaction became a minefield of potential judgment, each glance a potential source of pity or misunderstanding.

It was a mundane Tuesday when everything changed. Sarah was at the local grocery store, her movements mechanical, trying to avoid eye contact with other shoppers. Ethan was strapped to her chest, peaceful and content.

"He's beautiful," a voice said.

Sarah looked up, instinctively prepared to deflect what she assumed would be another pitying comment. Instead, she saw Lisa – a woman with kind eyes and a warm smile. Unlike other encounters, there was no awkward sympathy in her gaze, just genuine appreciation.

"Thank you," Sarah responded, her voice rusty from disuse.

Lisa's own son, Jason, sat in the shopping cart. Sarah noticed immediately that he seemed different – there was something unique about his features, a familiarity that made her heart race.

"Have you heard about the community centre's support group?" Lisa asked casually, as if discussing the weather. "They have a wonderful program for mothers of children with different abilities."

The phrase "different abilities" struck Sarah. It was so different from the narrative of limitation she had been telling herself.

Lisa scribbled down an address on a piece of paper. "No pressure," she said. "But sometimes, talking helps. And the community there – they understand in a way others can't."

That evening, as Ethan slept, Sarah stared at the address. The paper seemed to pulse with possibility – a lifeline she wasn't sure she was ready to grab, but desperately needed.

Her finger traced the address of the community centre. For the first time since the diagnosis, a tiny spark of hope flickered in her chest. She didn't know what awaited her, but something told her that this might be the first step towards understanding – not just the world's perception of Ethan, but her own.

The community centre bustled with quiet energy when Sarah first stepped inside, Ethan secured snugly in his baby carrier. Her fingers trembled slightly, gripping the diaper bag like a shield against uncertainty. The spacious room felt both intimidating and unexpectedly welcoming, with soft pastel walls adorned with artwork created by children with diverse abilities.

A warm-faced woman named Margaret, who coordinated the support group, approached Sarah with a gentle smile. "First time here?" she asked, her voice soft and understanding.

Sarah nodded; her initial nervousness evident in the way she shifted her weight from one foot to another. "I'm Sarah," she managed, "and this is Ethan."

Margaret guided her toward a semicircle of chairs where several women sat, each with their own children. Some were playing quietly, others engaged in various activities. The diversity was remarkable - children with different abilities, different backgrounds, yet united by a shared experience of navigating challenging journeys.

"Everyone here understands," Margaret whispered, sensing Sarah's apprehension. "This is a safe space."

As Sarah settled into a chair, the women began sharing their stories. There was Elena, whose daughter Maria had autism, and who spoke passionately about inclusive education. Rachel, whose son Jake had cerebral palsy, discussed the latest adaptive technologies that were helping her child communicate more effectively.

"When Jake first started using his communication device," Rachel shared, her eyes sparkling, "it was like watching a whole new world open up for him. He could finally tell us exactly what he was thinking."

These stories resonated deeply with Sarah. For the first time since Ethan's diagnosis, she didn't feel alone. These women weren't just sharing challenges; they were celebrating their children's unique strengths and potential.

Lisa, whom Sarah had met at the grocery store, sat nearby and caught her eye. She winked, a gesture of solidarity that made Sarah feel instantly more comfortable.

"We have resources," Margaret explained, spreading out pamphlets about early intervention programs, therapy options, and educational support. "The community centre offers weekly workshops, therapy sessions, and most importantly, a network of support."

Sarah learned about speech therapists specializing in working with children with Down syndrome, occupational therapy programs, and support groups specifically tailored to parents. Each piece of information felt like a lifeline, slowly replacing her earlier feelings of isolation with a sense of hope.

During a break, Elena approached Sarah. "Ethan is beautiful," she said, peeking at the sleeping baby. "How old is he?"

"Four months," Sarah responded, a hint of protective pride entering her voice. "He's already showing such curiosity."

The women around her nodded, sharing knowing smiles. They understood that "development" looked different for each child, and that difference didn't mean deficit.

As the meeting progressed, Sarah began to see a roadmap for her journey. These women weren't just surviving; they were thriving. They were advocates, researchers, fighters - transforming challenges into opportunities.

"The school system can be overwhelming," Rachel advised her. "But we've learned that early advocacy makes a massive difference. Start building your support network now."

Sarah listened intently, her perspective slowly shifting. The word "disability" began to feel less like a limitation and more like a different pathway of experiencing the world.

By the meeting's end, Sarah had collected contact information, resource guides, and most importantly, a sense of community. As she packed up Ethan, preparing to leave, she felt something she hadn't experienced since his diagnosis: genuine optimism.

Margaret approached her one last time. "Next week, we're discussing educational inclusion strategies. Would you like to join us?"

Sarah's smile was her answer - bright, hopeful, and filled with newfound strength.

The community centre had become more than a building. It was a beacon of understanding, a place where differences were celebrated, and potential was recognized in all its beautiful, unique forms.

The community centre buzzed with anticipation. Colourful posters lined the walls, announcing the upcoming talent showcase—an event that promised to be more than just a simple performance. For Sarah and the other mothers, it represented something profound: a celebration of their children's unique abilities.

Sarah watched Ethan practice his routine, her heart both nervous and proud. He was practicing a simple dance routine, his movements careful but determined. Lisa, who had become a close friend since that fateful grocery store encounter, stood beside her, offering quiet encouragement.

"He's doing great," Lisa whispered, placing a gentle hand on Sarah's shoulder. "Look how focused he is."

Indeed, Ethan's tongue poked out slightly in concentration, a gesture that made Sarah's heart swell. It was a far cry from the overwhelming fear and isolation she had felt when first receiving his diagnosis. The support group had transformed her perspective, showing her that different didn't mean less.

The rehearsals were a mosaic of experiences. Maria, whose son Jacob had autism, helped coordinate the backstage preparations. "It's not about perfection," she told the group during one practice session. "It's about celebration. These children have so much to show the world."

As the day of the showcase approached, Sarah's anxiety began to build. Despite the support of her newfound community, old fears still lingered. What if people stared? What if they didn't understand? What if Ethan struggled and became discouraged?

"You're overthinking again," Lisa said during their final practice session. She knew Sarah well enough now to recognize her spiral of worry. "These children are going to shine, Sarah. They're going to show everyone exactly who they are."

The other mothers nodded in solidarity. There was Elena, whose daughter Sophie had cerebral palsy, and Rachel, whose son Michael had a rare genetic condition. Each had their own story, their own challenges, but they shared a common bond—an unwavering love for their children and a determination to challenge societal perceptions.

On the morning of the showcase, Sarah helped Ethan into his specially chosen outfit—a bright blue shirt that made his eyes sparkle. Her hands trembled slightly as she adjusted his collar, a mixture of excitement and nervousness coursing through her.

"Ready, buddy?" she asked, her voice attempting to sound more confident than she felt.

Ethan grinned, a wide, uninhibited smile that momentarily dissolved all of Sarah's fears. "Ready, Mommy!" he declared.

The community centre was transformed. Chairs were arranged in a semicircle, decorated with balloons and streamers. Parents, siblings, and a few curious community members filled the space, creating an atmosphere of anticipation and support.

Behind the scenes, the mothers helped their children prepare. There were last-minute costume adjustments, whispered words of encouragement, and nervous giggles. Sarah caught Elena's eye and they shared a knowing smile—a silent communication that understood both the fear and the immense pride they were experiencing.

As the showcase began, each child took the stage with varying degrees of confidence. Some needed gentle encouragement, others bounded forward with unbridled enthusiasm. When Ethan's turn approached, Sarah felt her breath catch in her throat.

This moment, she realized, was about more than just a performance. It was a statement. A declaration that these children were not defined by their challenges, but by their extraordinary spirits.

The music started. Ethan took his first steps.

And in that moment, Sarah understood that this journey—their journey—was just beginning.

The community centre's small auditorium buzzed with anticipation. Rows of folding chairs were filled with parents, siblings, and friends, their faces a tapestry of hope and excitement. Sarah's hands trembled slightly as she sat near the front, her fingers intertwined, knuckles white with nervous energy.

The talent showcase had already featured several performances. A young girl with autism had played a mesmerizing piano piece, her fingers dancing across the keys with precision that took everyone's breath away. Another child had performed a sign language poetry recitation that moved several audience members to tears.

Now it was Ethan's turn.

Sarah caught Margaret's encouraging smile from the side of the stage. Her friend from the support group gave her a reassuring nod. Just weeks ago, Sarah would have been paralyzed with fear, imagining every possible way Ethan might be judged or misunderstood. But today, something felt different.

Ethan stepped onto the stage, wearing a bright blue shirt that Margaret had helped him pick out specifically for the showcase.

He looked small against the expansive stage, but there was a determination in his eyes that made Sarah's heart swell with pride.

The music began - a simple melody they had practiced together countless times. Ethan was performing a dance routine he had learned with the help of an inclusive dance program at the community centre. Each movement was carefully choreographed, each step a testament to his dedication and practice.

For the first few moments, Ethan moved with confidence. Then, unexpectedly, he stumbled. The music continued, but Ethan froze, his eyes wide with sudden uncertainty.

Sarah felt her breath catch. Years of internalized fear threatened to overwhelm her. Would people laugh? Would they see Ethan's momentary hesitation as a limitation? The old doubts crept in - the same fears that had once kept her isolated, afraid of the world's judgment.

But something remarkable happened.

From the audience, gentle encouragement began. "You've got this!" someone whispered. Another voice softly called, "Take your time!" These weren't sounds of pity, but of genuine support.

Lisa, who sat next to Sarah, gently squeezed her hand. "He's doing great," she whispered.

Ethan took a deep breath. His eyes scanned the audience and landed on Sarah. In that moment, their connection transcended words. Sarah's smile, filled with unconditional love and belief, seemed to restore his confidence.

He resumed the dance.

Each movement now carried more than just choreography. It was a statement - a beautiful, powerful declaration of his ability, his individuality. When the music ended, the auditorium erupted in applause.

But for Sarah, the real triumph wasn't in the performance. It was in the collective spirit of understanding that filled the room. These weren't just parents of children with disabilities. They were advocates, supporters, a community bound by love that saw beyond limitations.

After the showcase, the mothers gathered. Their conversations were filled with pride, shared experiences, and genuine joy. They talked about future plans, upcoming therapies, school challenges, and moments of unexpected triumph.

"Did you see how confidently Ethan recovered?" Margaret said to Sarah. "That's resilience. That's what matters."

Sarah realized something profound in that moment. The journey wasn't about achieving perfection. It was about embracing every moment, every challenge, every small victory. It was about understanding that differences weren't deficits - they were simply different expressions of human potential.

As they prepared to leave, Ethan tugged at her hand, his face beaming with the pure, unfiltered joy of a child who had just experienced something remarkable. And in that simple gesture, Sarah found her greatest lesson - love knows no boundaries, and potential has no single definition.

The talent showcase had been more than an event. It was a celebration of diversity, a testament to the power of community, and a beautiful reminder that every child, regardless of their abilities, deserves to shine.

The soft morning light filtered through the community centre's windows, casting a warm glow on the familiar faces Sarah had come to know over the past few months. Today's meeting felt different—more celebratory, more hopeful. The recent talent showcase had transformed something fundamental in their group, breaking down invisible barriers of doubt and isolation.

Sarah watched Ethan playing with the other children, his movements more confident, his smile broader than ever before. The showcase had been more than just a performance; it had been a turning point. She remembered the moment he'd stumbled during his dance, the brief flicker of uncertainty in his eyes—and how quickly that had transformed into determination.

"He's really come a long way," Margaret said, sitting down beside Sarah. The support group leader had been a constant source of wisdom and encouragement throughout Sarah's journey.

Sarah nodded, her eyes never leaving Ethan. "I never thought I'd say this a few months ago, but I'm proud of how far we've both come."

The mothers began discussing their plans for a monthly support network—something that had organically grown from their shared experiences. Lisa, who had first introduced Sarah to the group, was taking the lead in organizing their next meetup.

"We've realized we're stronger together," Lisa explained, her enthusiasm infectious. "Not just for ourselves, but for our children. Each of us brings a unique perspective, a different strength."

The conversation flowed naturally, touching on practical challenges—navigating school systems, finding appropriate therapies, advocating for their children's needs—but there was an underlying current of hope that hadn't existed before the talent showcase.

Sarah found herself reflecting on her initial fears. The diagnosis had once seemed like a mountain too steep to climb, a challenge that would define her entire existence. Now, she saw it differently. Ethan wasn't defined by his Down syndrome—he was defined by his spirit, his determination, his capacity for joy.

As the morning progressed, the children continued playing, their laughter a soundtrack to the mothers' conversations. Sarah noticed how naturally they interacted; how little they seemed to care about their differences. It was a powerful reminder of the pure, uncomplicated way children see the world.

"We're planning something special," Margaret announced to the group. "A quarterly community event that showcases not just talents, but the incredible journeys of our children and families."

The room buzzed with excitement. This was more than just an event—it was a statement. A declaration that their children were valuable, capable, and deserving of recognition.

When the meeting concluded, Sarah approached Margaret. "I want to help," she said firmly. "I want to be more involved in advocacy."

Margaret's smile was knowing. "I've been waiting for you to say that," she responded. "Your journey from isolation to empowerment is exactly what others need to see."

As they prepared to leave, Ethan ran up to Sarah, his face bright with excitement. "Mommy, can we practice my dance?" he asked, revealing the confidence he'd discovered during the showcase.

Sarah knelt down, meeting his excited gaze. "Absolutely," she said, hugging him tightly. In that moment, she realized the transformation wasn't just about Ethan—it was about her too. She had become not just his mother, but his strongest advocate.

The community centre, once a place of uncertainty, now felt like home. The network of support she'd discovered was more than just a group of mothers—it was a family, united by love, resilience, and an unwavering commitment to celebrating their children's unique abilities.

As they walked out, Sarah knew their journey was just beginning. But for the first time, she felt truly prepared—not with fear, but with hope, determination, and a profound sense of belonging.

CHAPTER TWENTY-ONE

BREAKING FREE

The morning sunlight filtered through the dusty windows of the small school office, casting long shadows across Jeeva's weary face. Her fingers moved methodically across the worn ledger, each entry a careful testament to her dedication. Around her, the silence was punctuated only by the occasional scrape of her pen and the distant sounds of children's laughter from the school playground.

Jeeva's mind was a whirlwind of thoughts. The upcoming arranged marriage hung over her like a heavy cloud, its weight compounded by the precarious nature of her job. Father Mathew, the school's director, had been increasingly critical, his disapproving glances growing more frequent with each passing week.

She remembered the conversation with her sisters just the previous evening. Priya, the eldest, had been particularly vocal. "The wedding is in two months," she had said, her tone a mixture of concern and urgency. "We need to ensure everything is prepared. Have you saved enough?"

The question echoed in Jeeva's mind. Saved enough? The very thought was a painful reminder of their family's constant struggle. Their father's alcoholism had drained their resources for years, leaving Jeeva as the primary breadwinner.

A sharp knock interrupted her thoughts. Father Mathew stood in the doorway, his imposing figure blocking the light. "Jeeva," he said, his voice stern, "I need to review the school's financial records.

Again."

She knew what this meant. Another scrutiny, another opportunity for him to find fault. Her hands trembled slightly as she gathered the documents, memories of previous confrontations flooding her mind.

Her thoughts drifted to her mother – a gentle soul who had passed away when Jeeva was just a teenager. She had been the buffer, the one who had protected Jeeva and her sisters from their father's volatile moods. Now, Jeeva carried that responsibility.

The family home was a testament to their struggles. Walls that once echoed with her mother's gentle singing now bore the marks of her father's alcoholic rages. Yet, beneath the pain, there was love – complicated, bruised, but present.

"Is something wrong?" Father Mathew's voice cut through her reverie.

"No, Father," Jeeva responded quickly, her voice steady despite the turbulence inside her. "Just preparing the documents you requested."

As she handed over the files, she caught a glimpse of her reflection in the window. A young woman on the cusp of a significant life change, carrying the weight of her family's expectations, her own dreams, and the constant fear of job insecurity.

That evening, as she prepared dinner for her father, the tension was palpable. He sat at the table, his hands shaking slightly – a remnant of his ongoing battle with alcohol. "The wedding," he mumbled, "it will solve everything."

Jeeva knew what he meant. The arranged marriage was more than just a traditional ceremony. It was a potential lifeline, a chance for financial stability. Her sisters had similar hopes, their conversations always circling back to how this marriage could change their fortunes.

But something inside Jeeva resisted. She wanted more than just survival. She wanted purpose, independence, respect.

As the night drew in, she found herself staring at her wedding gown – carefully saved and prepared. Each piece represented a compromise, a negotiation between her dreams and her family's expectations.

The upcoming family meeting weighed heavily on her mind. Discussion of dowry, arrangements, expectations – all would be dissected, analysed. And through it all, Jeeva would need to maintain her composure, her resilience.

She thought about the priest, about her job, about the marriage. Each represented a different form of authority, each demanding conformity. But something was changing within her – a spark of resistance, of self-worth that refused to be extinguished.

As she prepared for bed, Jeeva's mind was a complex tapestry of emotions – fear, hope, determination. The wedding was approaching. Her job hung by a thread. Her family's future balanced precariously.

But she was ready to fight. For herself. For her dreams. For a future she would define.

The night settled around her, holding the promise of challenges yet to come, and the potential of transformation waiting just beyond the horizon.

The morning sunlight filtered through the dusty convent windows, casting long shadows across the sparse dormitory where young Jeeva once lived. Memories cascaded like water droplets, each one carrying the weight of forgotten dreams and silent struggles.

Jeeva's mind drifted back to those formative years, her small frame hunched over worn textbooks, determined to create a future different from the one her family seemed destined to repeat. The absence of her mother hung like a persistent ghost, a void that had shaped her resilience from an early age.

She remembered the day everything changed. Twelve-year-old Jeeva had stood by the window, watching her father stumble home, the familiar smell of alcohol preceding his arrival. Her mother, gentle and worn, would prepare a meal in silence, her eyes holding a mixture of resignation and hope. When her mother fell ill, Jeeva became the unexpected pillar of strength for her family.

"You must be strong," her mother had whispered during her final days, her hand weakly clutching Jeeva's. Those words became a mantra, etched into the deepest recesses of her heart.

The convent had been her sanctuary. Sister Margaret, a kind-faced nun who supervised the dormitory, had recognized Jeeva's potential. "Education is your path," she would say, noting how Jeeva devoured every book she could find, her hunger for knowledge a stark contrast to the limitations imposed by her circumstances.

In the present, Jeeva's fingers traced the edges of an old photograph – a younger version of herself, standing proudly in her school uniform, her sisters flanking her. Priya and Asha, though younger, had always looked up to her. Their relationship was complex – a blend of love, dependency, and the unspoken pressure of familial expectations.

The memories of the convent blended with her current reality. The local school where she now worked felt both familiar and constraining. The priest who ran the school represented a different kind of authority – bureaucratic and unyielding, yet not as directly oppressive as her past.

"We're worried about you," Priya had said during their last conversation. "The wedding is our only chance to improve our situation."

Asha had nodded in agreement, her eyes reflecting a mixture of hope and desperation. They weren't malicious; they were simply trapped in the same cycle of survival that had defined their family for generations.

Jeeva's reflection deepened. The upcoming wedding was more than just a personal milestone – it was a potential lifeline for her family. Yet, something within her resisted the complete surrender to this predetermined path.

The priest at the school embodied the institutional pressures that seemed to define her existence. His constant scrutiny, the endless paperwork, the seemingly arbitrary rules – they all contributed to a sense of contained rebellion brewing within her.

As the day progressed, Jeeva found herself caught between her past and present. The ghosts of her childhood – her mother's gentle guidance, her father's struggling alcoholism, the convent's structured hope – all converged in this moment of anticipation.

Her sisters' voices echoed in her mind. Their concerns were genuine, their love unconditional. They saw the wedding as a solution, while Jeeva saw it as another challenge to navigate.

A soft sigh escaped her lips. The confrontation with her sisters was inevitable. Their perspectives, shaped by similar experiences yet fundamentally different, would soon clash. But for now, Jeeva allowed herself to be suspended in this moment of reflection, gathering strength from the memories that had formed her.

The photograph of her younger self seemed to whisper, "You are more than your circumstances. You are your own story."

As evening approached, Jeeva prepared herself. The ghosts of her past were not chains, but stepping stones. And she was ready to step forward, one careful, determined step at a time.

The morning light filtered through the dusty school windows, casting long shadows across the hallway where Jeeva stood, her fingers tracing the edge of her worn clipboard. Today was different. Today, she would confront the priest who had been systematically undermining her position and threatening her livelihood.

Her heart raced with a mixture of fear and determination. The memories of her past—the struggles with her alcoholic father, the loss of her mother, the constant pressure from her sisters—had all converged into this moment. She had spent years surviving, but now she was ready to truly live.

Father Mathew was in his office, a small, austere room that always smelled of old books and stale incense. Jeeva knocked firmly, her hand steady despite the trembling in her chest.

"Enter," came the curt response.

She stepped inside, her posture straighter than she had ever held it before. The priest looked up, his weathered face a mask of bureaucratic indifference.

"Father," Jeeva began, her voice clear and controlled, "we need to discuss my position at the school."

The priest raised an eyebrow, a gesture that had intimidated her countless times before. But not today.

"I've noticed the recent changes in my work assignments," she continued. "The constant scrutiny, the reduced responsibilities, the subtle hints about my future here. I'm aware these are attempts to push me out."

Father Mathew leaned back, his fingers intertwined. "Miss Jeeva, the school has certain standards—"

"Standards?" she interrupted, a spark of defiance in her eyes. "These standards seem to apply only to certain employees. I've been dedicated to this institution, worked overtime, covered additional responsibilities. My performance has been consistently excellent."

The confrontation was everything she had rehearsed in her mind. Each word was a deliberate strike against the institutional oppression she had endured. Her sisters' voices echoed in her mind—Priya's practical concerns, Asha's emotional support—but this moment was entirely her own.

Father Mathew's demeanour shifted. The patronizing smile disappeared, replaced by a look of genuine surprise. No one, especially not a young woman on the verge of an arranged marriage, had ever spoken to him in this manner.

"I am not asking for special treatment," Jeeva said, her voice steady. "I am demanding fair treatment. My upcoming marriage does not diminish my professional capabilities. If anything, it represents another dimension of my life's journey."

The priest remained silent, a rare occurrence that spoke volumes.

Jeeva continued, drawing strength from her years at the convent, from Sister Margaret's teachings about self-worth and dignity. "I know the challenges of this institution. I understand the pressures. But I will not be marginalized or made to feel lesser because of my gender or my personal circumstances."

A moment of profound silence filled the room. Father Mathew seemed to be reassessing the young woman before him—no longer just another clerk, but a force to be reckoned with.

"Your candidness is... unexpected," he finally said.

"My candidness is necessary," Jeeva responded.

As she left the office, a complex mix of emotions swept through her. She had confronted an authority figure who had symbolized institutional power throughout her life. The act was more than just a professional stand—it was a personal liberation.

Her sisters would be surprised. Her father would likely be indifferent. But Jeeva knew this moment was about her—her voice, her dignity, her future.

Outside the office, the school buzzed with its usual morning activities. But something had changed. Jeeva walked differently, her steps deliberate, her spirit unbroken.

The confrontation was just the beginning. Her real journey of self-discovery and empowerment was just unfolding.

The morning light filtered through the small window of Jeeva's modest room, casting a soft glow on her contemplative face. The confrontation with the priest still echoed in her mind—a testament to her newfound courage. She traced her fingers along the delicate embroidery of her wedding sari, a complex tapestry of emotions weaving through her thoughts.

Her father sat in the adjacent room, the silence between them heavy with unspoken words. Today would be different. Today, she would bridge the chasm that had separated them for years.

Jeeva took a deep breath and entered the room where her father sat, his weathered hands trembling slightly as he held a cup of tea. The smell of alcohol lingered faintly—a ghost of his past struggles.

"Appa," she began, her voice soft but steady, "we need to talk."

Her father looked up, a mixture of apprehension and curiosity in his eyes. Years of pain, disappointment, and unresolved emotions hung in the air between them.

"I know my life hasn't been easy," she continued, sitting beside him. "Your struggles with alcohol, the challenges we faced—they've shaped me more than you might realize."

To her surprise, her father's eyes glistened. The rigid exterior he had maintained for years began to crack. "I never meant to burden you, Jeeva," he whispered, his voice breaking. "After your mother left, I felt like I was drowning."

For the first time, Jeeva saw her father not as an oppressive figure, but as a vulnerable human being. The conversation flowed, raw and honest. They discussed his alcoholism, her childhood, the weight of expectations that had crushed them both.

"I'm getting married," Jeeva said, "but not because it's what everyone expects. I'm choosing this path because I believe it can be a new beginning—for me, and for our family."

Her sisters, Priya and Asha, had been supportive since her confrontation with the priest. They understood now that Jeeva's resistance wasn't rebellion, but a quest for genuine self-determination.

The wedding preparations continued, but with a different energy. Where once they felt like chains, they now seemed like carefully chosen decorations of her own design. Jeeva had secured her position at the school, standing up to the priest's oppressive leadership. Her job was no longer a source of constant anxiety but a platform for her growing confidence.

As the wedding day approached, Jeeva reflected on her journey. The convent where she'd found her first glimpses of hope, the challenging years of supporting her family, the moments of doubt—they had all led her here.

Her conversation with her father had been a turning point. He had apologized for his past, acknowledged her strength, and for the first time, truly saw her as an individual with her own dreams and capabilities.

The evening before her wedding, Jeeva sat with her sisters. They shared a moment of quiet understanding—no longer bound by mere survival, but united by genuine love and mutual respect.

"I'm proud of you," Priya said, squeezing her hand. "You've shown us that our stories aren't written by others, but by ourselves."

Asha nodded, adding, "You've changed everything for our family."

Jeeva smiled, a blend of hope and determination reflecting in her eyes. The wedding wasn't an end, but a beginning. A chance to create her own narrative, to break cycles of oppression, and to build a future on her own terms.

As the night settled, she thought about the priest, about her father, about the countless expectations she had navigated. She had learned that resilience wasn't about never breaking, but about how beautifully one could rebuild.

Tomorrow, she would step into a new chapter—not as a victim of circumstances, but as the author of her own story.

The room was quiet, but her spirit resonated with a powerful, unbreakable hope.

CHAPTER TWENTY-TWO

FROM GAZE TO GRACE

The morning sunlight streamed through the classroom windows of Westfield Urban High School, casting long shadows across the freshly cleaned linoleum floor. Emily Carter adjusted the collar of her navy-blue blazer, her fingers tracing a subtle pattern of nervousness beneath the crisp fabric. At twenty-five, she was no stranger to challenges, but this was different. This was her first full-time teaching position, and she was determined to make a difference.

The classroom was her canvas. Carefully selected quotes from diverse authors adorned the walls - Chimamanda Ngozi Adichie, James Baldwin, Maya Angelou - each carefully chosen to inspire and provoke thought. Emily believed in the power of words, in their ability to transform perspectives and challenge existing narratives.

Growing up in a working-class family in the suburbs, Emily had always been the one to speak up, to question, to challenge. Her mother, a factory worker who had fought her way through gender discrimination, had instilled in her a deep sense of resilience. "Your voice matters," she would tell Emily, “Even when others try to silence you."

As the students began to file in, Emily noticed the diverse mix. Urban teenagers with their varied backgrounds, styles, and attitudes filled the classroom. Some looked disinterested, others curious, a few challenging. She recognized the dynamic immediately - this wasn't just about teaching English literature; this was about creating a space of mutual respect and understanding.

"Good morning," she announced, her voice clear and confident. "I'm Ms. Carter, and this is Advanced English Literature."

A low murmur ran through the classroom. Jake Rodriguez, seated near the back, caught her eye. There was something different about him - a mix of admiration and uncertainty that intrigued her. Unlike some of his peers who seemed dismissive, Jake seemed genuinely interested.

During the staff meeting later that morning, Emily got her first real taste of the school's internal dynamics. The staff room was a cacophony of conversations, coffee machines humming, and the subtle undercurrents of professional politics.

Mr. Thompson, the history teacher, epitomized a certain type of educator Emily had encountered before. Charismatic, apparently well-liked, but with an underlying current of casual sexism that made her skin prickle.

"Well, well," he said, his voice carrying across the room, "looks like we've got a fresh face. Welcome to the trenches, Ms. Carter."

The comment was loaded, designed to test her reaction. Emily knew this game. She'd seen it played out countless times in her previous teaching experiences and internships.

"Thank you, Mr. Thompson," she responded evenly, maintaining direct eye contact. "I'm looking forward to contributing to the school community."

Nearby, Sarah Martinez, another young teacher, gave her a knowing smile. During a quick break, Sarah approached her.

"First day survival tip," Sarah whispered, "don't let them see you sweat."

Sarah had been through similar experiences. As a Latina teacher in an urban school, she understood the subtle and not-so-subtle challenges of navigating institutional dynamics.

"Thompson can be... challenging," Sarah continued. "But you seem like you can handle yourself."

The day progressed with a mixture of excitement and underlying tension. Emily's literature class discussed "To Kill a Mockingbird", using the text to explore themes of systemic prejudice and individual courage. Jake's insights particularly impressed her - he seemed to grasp the deeper nuances of racial and social dynamics.

By the end of the day, Emily felt a complex mix of emotions. Excitement about her potential impact, frustration at the existing power structures, and a steely determination to create meaningful change. As she packed her bag, surrounded by stacks of essays and lesson plans, she reflected on her mother's words. Her voice mattered. And in this school, she was going to ensure it was heard.

Little did she know how prophetic those thoughts would become.

The fluorescent lights of the teachers‘ lounge flickered with a harsh intensity that matched the tension brewing in Emily's shoulders. The inappropriate joke Mr. Thompson had made during the staff meeting still rang in her ears, a poisonous echo that seemed to challenge her very presence in the school.

She clutched her coffee mug, her knuckles white, watching the way some of the male teachers exchanged knowing glances. It wasn't just the joke itself, but the casual manner in which it had been delivered—as if her discomfort was something to be expected, even accepted.

"You, okay?" Sarah's voice cut through her thoughts. The older teacher sat down beside Emily, her eyes knowing and sympathetic.

Emily took a deep breath. "Have you ever felt like you're constantly fighting just to be taken seriously?"

Sarah's laugh was dry, tinged with years of experience. "Welcome to teaching, especially in a school like this. It's not about being good at your job—it's about proving you belong."

The conversation was interrupted by a group of students passing by the lounge window. Among them was Jake, one of her more promising students. She noticed him initially holding back from a crude conversation, then slowly being drawn in by peer pressure—laughing nervously at jokes that made him visibly uncomfortable.

That afternoon's English class became a battleground of subtle tensions. Emily could feel the undercurrent of disrespect from some of the male students—whispered comments, barely concealed snickers, looks that lingered just a moment too long.

"Today," she announced, her voice cutting through the ambient noise, "we're going to discuss communication and respect."

The room fell silent. Not the respectful silence of engaged students, but the wary silence of those anticipating confrontation.

Jake shifted uncomfortably in his seat. Emily recognized the conflict in his eyes—a desire to be respectful warring with the overwhelming pressure to conform to toxic masculinity.

"Mr. Thompson's joke wasn't just inappropriate," Emily continued, choosing her words carefully. "It represents a larger problem of how women are perceived and treated in professional spaces."

A few students looked down. Others exchanged uncomfortable glances. One student, Marcus, muttered something under his breath.

"Something you'd like to share with the class?" Emily's voice was calm but firm.

Marcus, caught off guard, mumbled, "Nothing, Ms. Carter."

After class, Jake approached her desk, looking conflicted. "Ms. Carter, I... I wanted to say I'm sorry. About how some guys act."

Emily softened her approach. "It takes courage to stand against peer pressure, Jake. Remember, respecting someone isn't about being perfect. It's about listening and trying to understand."

The day wore on, each interaction a subtle negotiation of boundaries. In the administrative office, Emily overheard hushed conversations—some supportive, some dismissive. The school's culture was a complex web of unspoken rules and ingrained behaviours.

That evening, she sat in her small apartment, grading papers and reflecting on the day. The challenges seemed insurmountable, but her determination burned bright. This wasn't just about her—it was about creating a space where every student could feel respected and heard.

Her phone buzzed. A text from Sarah: "Dinner tomorrow? We should talk strategy."

Emily smiled. She wasn't alone in this fight.

The incident with Mr. Thompson had been more than just a moment of inappropriate humour. It was a line in the sand—a challenge that Emily was prepared to meet head-on. Her resilience wasn't just a personal trait; it was becoming a powerful tool for change.

As the city outside her window hummed with evening energy, Emily began drafting notes for a workshop. Something that would challenge the current culture, spark genuine dialogue, and create real change.

The first step towards empowerment, she knew, was refusing to be silenced.

The conference room buzzed with nervous energy as Emily arranged the chairs in a circular formation, her hands trembling slightly but her posture resolute. She had spent weeks planning this workshop on professionalism and respect, carefully crafting a presentation that would challenge the toxic culture embedded within Westfield Urban High School.

Sarah had been her strongest ally throughout the preparation. "Are you sure you want to do this?" she had asked during lunch earlier that week, her voice a mix of concern and admiration. Emily had nodded, her eyes reflecting a determination that brooked no argument.

The morning of the workshop arrived with an underlying tension. Mr. Thompson had caught wind of Emily's plans and had been circulating passive-aggressive comments in the staff room. "Some young teachers think they can change everything," he'd muttered loudly enough for Emily to hear, his sardonic laugh cutting through the morning's ambient noise.

As students and staff began filing into the room, Emily noticed Jake Rodriguez sitting near the back, looking both curious and apprehensive. Their eyes met briefly, and she saw a flicker of support in his gaze. He had been quietly observing her journey, understanding more than most the complexities of challenging institutional culture.

"Good morning," Emily began, her voice clear and steady. "Today, we're going to have a conversation about respect, professionalism, and creating an environment where everyone feels valued."

She started with personal narratives—stories from her mother's experiences with workplace discrimination, excerpts from powerful women who had challenged systemic barriers. The room grew progressively quieter, the usual teenage chatter replaced by an unexpected attentiveness.

Mr. Thompson sat in the back, arms crossed, his body language radiating disapproval. But Emily didn't let his presence deter her. She methodically deconstructed casual sexism, explaining how seemingly minor comments could create hostile environments.

"Objectification isn't a compliment," she explained, her voice gaining strength. "It's a form of dehumanization that reduces individuals to mere objects of desire or ridicule."

A few male students shifted uncomfortably. Some looked defensive, others contemplative. Jake raised his hand. "Can you give us specific examples of how these behaviours manifest?" he asked, his question genuine and thoughtful.

Emily appreciated his support. She shared scenarios—inappropriate comments, dismissive attitudes, subtle forms of marginalization. She wasn't just lecturing; she was inviting dialogue, creating a space for genuine reflection.

The workshop's most powerful moment came unexpectedly. A female student named Maria, typically quiet, stood up. "This happens more often than people realize," she said, her voice trembling but determined. "In class, in hallways, everywhere."

Her testimony sparked a ripple of murmurs, then conversations. Students began sharing experiences, supporting each other. The hierarchical teacher-student dynamic dissolved momentarily, replaced by a collective understanding.

Mr. Thompson's discomfort was palpable. When Emily directly addressed workplace harassment, referencing subtle professional microaggressions, he looked increasingly agitated. She wasn't targeting him specifically, but her words cut precisely through normalized toxic behaviours.

By workshop's end, something had shifted. The room felt different—charged with potential, with the electricity of uncomfortable but necessary conversations.

Principal Rodriguez, who had been observing silently, approached Emily afterward. "That was... unexpectedly powerful," he admitted, a newfound respect in his tone.

Sarah squeezed Emily's shoulder. "You did it," she whispered.

But Emily knew this was just the beginning. One workshop couldn't dismantle years of ingrained behaviour. Yet, it was a crucial first step—a crack in the wall of indifference, allowing light to penetrate.

As students filed out, Jake lingered. "Thank you," he said simply. "For showing us there's a different way to interact."

Emily smiled, understanding that true change happens not through grand gestures, but through persistent, compassionate education. One conversation at a time.

The workshop might have been just two hours, but its reverberations would echo through Westfield Urban High School for much longer.

The morning sunlight filtered through the school's windows, casting a soft glow on the hallways that seemed to symbolize the change brewing within Westfield Urban High School. Emily Carter stood in her classroom, reviewing the documentation of the workshop's impact—a stack of emails, meeting notes, and proposed policy changes that represented more than just paper. They were proof of possibility.

Principal Rodriguez had been surprisingly receptive in the weeks following the workshop. What began as a potential disciplinary conversation had transformed into a collaborative effort to reshape the school's culture. Emily traced her fingers along the quotes that still adorned her classroom walls—words of resilience from Audre Lorde, Maya Angelou, and bell hooks—each a testament to the power of speaking truth.

Her conversation with Jake had been a turning point. After the workshop, he had approached her with genuine remorse, sharing how the discussions had made him reconsider his previous behaviours. "I never realized how much my silence contributed to the problem," he had admitted, his voice tinged with a maturity that went beyond his years.

Sarah entered the classroom, a cup of coffee in hand. "How are you holding up?" she asked, understanding the weight of the past few weeks.

Emily smiled, a mixture of exhaustion and triumph in her eyes. "It's been challenging, but I'm starting to see real change. The student council is drafting a new code of conduct, and several departments are implementing mandatory respect workshops."

The resistance hadn't completely disappeared. Mr. Thompson had been quietly transferred to an administrative position, a compromise that felt both satisfying and insufficient. Emily knew that true change was more complex than simply removing one problematic individual.

A knock at the door interrupted their conversation. Maria, the quiet student who had spoken so powerfully during the workshop, entered hesitantly. "Ms. Carter," she said, her voice stronger than Emily had ever heard it before, "I wanted to show you something."

She handed Emily a folder. Inside were drafts of a student-led initiative on creating a more inclusive school environment. Peer support groups, mentorship programs, and communication workshops—Maria and her classmates had taken the workshop's lessons and transformed them into actionable plans.

"We want to make sure this doesn't just become another forgotten moment," Maria explained. "We want real change."

Emily felt a lump in her throat. This was why she had become a teacher—not just to teach literature, but to help students find their voices, to empower them to create the world they wanted to see.

The resolution wasn't perfect. There would still be challenges, still be moments of doubt and resistance. But as Emily looked around her classroom—at the quotes, the student initiatives, the small but significant signs of progress—she recognized the power of resilience.

"We're creating something important," she told Sarah and Maria. "It's not about winning against someone, but about creating a space where everyone can succeed."

As the day progressed, Emily reflected on her journey. She thought of her mother, who had fought similar battles in her own workplace decades ago. The change was slow, but it was happening. Each conversation, each workshop, each moment of standing up and speaking out was a step toward a more equitable future.

The bell rang, signalling the end of the day. But for Emily, it felt like just the beginning.

Outside her classroom, the hallways bustled with students—their conversations more respectful, their interactions more aware. Jake waved as he passed, no longer part of a problematic group dynamic but as an individual committed to growth.

Emily knew the work was far from over. But for the first time since starting at Westfield, she felt truly hopeful. Resilience wasn't about never facing challenges—it was about facing them with courage, compassion, and an unwavering belief in the possibility of change.

Her mother's words echoed in her mind: "Your voice is your most powerful tool. Never stop using it."

And she wouldn't. Not today. Not ever.

CHAPTER TWENTY-THREE

ECHOES OF RESILIENCE

The morning sunlight filtered through the slightly dusty windows of Willowbrook Residential Care Home, casting long shadows across the worn linoleum floor. Evelyn Matthews sat in her usual spot by the window, her weathered hands folded neatly in her lap, watching the world outside with eyes that had seen decades of change.

Willowbrook was a modest facility, nestled in a quiet suburban neighbourhood. Its pale-yellow walls and faded floral curtains spoke of years of service, of countless stories and lives that had passed through its corridors. The common room was a testament to the residents‘ collective history - a mismatched collection of armchairs, side tables, and memories.

Evelyn's sharp gaze surveyed the room. Harold Jenkins sat in his wheelchair near the television, his hands trembling slightly as he tried to adjust the remote. Maria Rodriguez was tucked into a corner, her eyes distant, seemingly lost in a world of her own memories. George Taylor was attempting to read a newspaper, squinting through thick glasses that seemed to slip down his nose with each passing moment.

The monotony of their morning was about to be interrupted.

"Excuse me," a soft voice announced, "I'm Emma Thompson. I'll be joining your community."

All heads turned. Emma stood at the doorway, a small suitcase by her side, her silver hair neatly pulled back, eyes scanning the room with a mixture of apprehension and determination. She was younger than most residents, perhaps in her early sixties, with a posture that suggested she wasn't entirely comfortable with her new surroundings.

Evelyn was the first to move. "Well, hello there," she called out, her voice crisp and welcoming. "I'm Evelyn. Would you like to sit down?"

Something in Evelyn's approach was different from her usual reserved demeanour. Perhaps it was Emma's uncertain expression, or the way she seemed slightly lost, that triggered a maternal instinct Evelyn thought she'd long since buried.

Harold shifted uncomfortably in his wheelchair. "New residents always disrupt everything," he muttered, just loud enough to be heard.

Maria remained silent; her gaze still fixed on some distant point beyond the room's walls.

George folded his newspaper, curiosity piquing through his usual disinterest. "Where are you from, Emma?" he asked, adjusting his glasses.

Emma hesitated, then sat in an empty armchair. "I'm from the city. My children... well, they thought it would be best if I had more support." The last words hung in the air, laden with unspoken emotions - a mix of hurt, resignation, and a barely concealed pain of perceived abandonment.

Evelyn recognized that pain. She had lived it herself for years.

"Support comes in many forms," Evelyn said softly, leaning forward. "Sometimes it's not about what your family decides, but about what you choose for yourself."

The staff nurse, Margaret, entered with Emma's paperwork. "Emma will be joining our morning activities," she announced cheerfully, seemingly oblivious to the complex emotional landscape of the room.

As the day progressed, Emma tried to settle in. She unpacked her few personal belongings - a photograph of what seemed to be her children, a well-worn novel, a soft blue cardigan. Each item was placed with care, as if each represented a fragment of a life she was leaving behind.

Evelyn watched her, a familiar ache of loneliness resonating within her. She recognized in Emma a kindred spirit - someone thrust into a new world, expected to adapt, to make peace with a life that felt increasingly smaller.

By afternoon, the initial tension had slightly softened. Harold had grudgingly offered Emma a section of his newspaper. Maria had occasionally glanced in her direction. George had asked about her reading preferences.

And Evelyn? She had decided that Emma would not be another resident who would fade into the background of Willowbrook. Something about her sparked a renewed sense of purpose in the old woman.

As evening approached, the residents gathered for dinner. The dining hall buzzed with a newfound energy - the energy of curiosity, of potential connection.

Emma looked around, a tentative smile forming. She was here. She would survive. And perhaps, just perhaps, she might find something unexpected in this place of endings and new beginnings.

Little did they know how profoundly Emma's arrival would change each of their lives.

The morning sunlight filtered through the worn curtains of Willowbrook, casting soft shadows across the common room where the residents were beginning to stir. Emma sat near the large bay window, her hands wrapped around a steaming mug of tea, feeling the cautious eyes of the other residents studying her with a mixture of curiosity and hesitation.

Harold was the first to approach her that morning, his movements slow and deliberate. His weathered hands gripped a wooden walking stick, each step a careful negotiation with his aging body. "Mind if I sit?" he asked, his voice gravelly but kind.

Emma smiled and gestured to the chair beside her. As Harold settled down, she could see the subtle tension in his shoulders – the complex dance of pride and vulnerability that comes with physical limitations. "How long have you been at Willowbrook?" she asked, sensing his need to be seen beyond his physical challenges.

Harold's eyes softened. "Three years now," he replied, "Though some days it feels like three decades." He shared stories of his past – a former carpenter whose hands had once crafted intricate furniture, now struggling to hold a simple tea cup steady. Emma listened intently, recognizing the profound loss he was navigating.

Nearby, Maria watched their interaction from across the room, her fingers nervously pleating the edge of her cardigan. Her past hung around her like a heavy cloak – years of unspoken pain and isolation that kept her at a careful distance from the others. Yet something about Emma's gentle presence seemed to draw her slightly closer.

George, always observant, saw an opportunity. He approached Emma with a chess set, his eyes twinkling with a renewed sense of purpose. "Care for a game?" he asked, a hint of his former competitive spirit evident in his voice. Emma agreed, and soon they were engaged in a gentle battle of wits, with George sharing snippets of his life – a retired professor who had never quite let go of his love for intellectual challenge.

Evelyn, true to her nature, orchestrated these interactions with a subtle but deliberate hand. She understood the delicate art of building community, of helping wounded souls find connection. During a group activity, she nudged Maria into conversation, creating small, manageable moments of interaction that didn't overwhelm.

"I used to paint," Maria whispered almost inaudibly during a craft session, her first voluntary share in months. Emma's gentle encouragement – a soft smile, an attentive ear – seemed to unlock something within her. Slowly, Maria began to reveal fragments of her story: a life marked by loss, a marriage that had crumbled under the weight of unspoken traumas.

The afternoon group discussion, typically a routine affair, took on a different tone with Emma's presence. Staff members noticed the subtle shift – residents who had previously sat in silent resignation now leaned slightly forward, engaged and curious.

Harold shared about his struggle with mobility, his voice cracking with vulnerability. "Some days, I feel invisible," he admitted. "Like my worth disappeared the moment I could no longer work with my hands."

Emma's response was immediate and genuine. "But your hands created beautiful things," she said. "That skill, that creativity – it doesn't vanish just because your body has changed."

These moments of connection were fragile, like delicate threads being carefully woven into a new tapestry. Each resident was learning to trust again, to believe that vulnerability could be met with compassion rather than judgment.

As evening approached, the common room hummed with a newfound energy. Conversations that would have been impossible weeks ago now flowed naturally. Emma had become more than just a new resident – she was a catalyst, a gentle force that was slowly transforming the emotional landscape of Willowbrook.

Evelyn watched the scene, a knowing smile playing on her lips. She understood that true healing happens in community, in those small, seemingly insignificant moments of human connection.

The day concluded with a sense of tentative hope. For the first time in years, the residents of Willowbrook felt something they had almost forgotten – the warmth of belonging.

The soft morning light filtered through the windows of Willowbrook, casting a warm glow on the faces of the residents gathered in the common room. Emma Thompson sat at the centre of a makeshift planning committee, her eyes sparkling with excitement as Evelyn, Harold, Maria, and George huddled around her, their voices a hushed blend of anticipation and careful strategy.

"We need to make this birthday surprise absolutely perfect," Evelyn declared, her sharp wit cutting through the morning's quiet. She pulled out a meticulously folded piece of paper – a hand-drawn chart of their surprise party plans.

Harold chuckled, his arthritic hands struggling to hold a pencil. "Perfect? With our bunch? That's asking for a miracle." Despite his words, there was a twinkle in his eye that betrayed his genuine excitement.

Maria, typically reserved, surprised everyone by suggesting decorations. "I used to be quite good at crafting," she said softly, her fingers tracing imaginary designs on the table. The admission was a rare glimpse into her guarded past, a small window of vulnerability that the others recognized as precious.

George, who had been quietly listening, suddenly perked up. "I know the kitchen staff," he whispered conspiratorially. "I can help smuggle out a birthday cake without Emma suspecting a thing."

The planning was more than just a birthday celebration. It was a lifeline – a collective effort that gave each resident a sense of purpose. For Evelyn, it was a chance to orchestrate something meaningful. For Harold, an opportunity to contribute despite his physical limitations. For Maria, a moment to reconnect with her forgotten creative side. For George, a way to feel useful again.

But their carefully laid plans were about to be challenged.

Mr. Richardson, the facility's administrator, called a meeting that afternoon. His announcement was a cold splash of reality. "Due to budget constraints," he began, his voice clinical and detached, "we'll be reducing funding for communal activities and group events."

The room fell silent. Emma looked around, seeing the hope drain from her newfound friends‘ faces. Evelyn's shoulders squared – a signal that she was preparing for battle.

"Absolutely not," Evelyn interrupted, her voice cutting through the administrator's monotone. "These activities are not luxuries. They're essential to the residents' mental and emotional well-being."

Harold wheeled himself forward, joining Evelyn. Maria, usually silent, found her voice. "We may be old," she said, her typically trembling voice now steady, "but we're not invisible."

George stood beside them, an unexpected united front that surprised even themselves.

Emma watched in awe as her friends transformed. These weren't just residents of an old age home – they were a community, fighting for their right to connection, to meaning, to joy.

The administrator, clearly unprepared for such unified resistance, stammered through his arguments. But the residents were relentless. They shared stories – how these activities were their lifeline, their reason for getting up each morning.

By the meeting's end, Mr. Richardson agreed to reconsider the budget cuts, promising a comprehensive review.

That evening, their planned surprise party for Emma took on a deeper significance. It was no longer just a celebration, but a testament to their newfound strength, their ability to fight together.

As Emma walked into the common room, expecting another ordinary evening, she was met with a burst of colour, streamers, and the collective cheer of her friends. Tears welled in her eyes – not of sadness, but of profound gratitude.

"We did this together," Evelyn whispered, squeezing Emma's hand.

The cake – slightly lopsided but made with genuine love – sat centrepiece. Around it, five individuals who had once felt alone now formed a tight-knit circle of support.

In that moment, Willowbrook was more than just a residential care home. It was home – in every sense of the word.

As the evening wound down and laughter echoed through the halls, each resident carried with them a renewed sense of hope. They had discovered something far more valuable than any planned activity – they had found each other.

CHAPTER TWENTY-FOUR

BREAKING THE STEREOTYPES

The morning sunlight spilled across the small kitchen, casting a warm glow on Lavanya's hands as they trembled slightly around the pregnancy test. Two pink lines. Definitive. Unmistakable. She was pregnant.

At thirty-two, Lavanya had waited longer than most of her friends to get married. Sarang had seemed different from the other men she'd met—thoughtful, kind, with a gentle smile that made her feel safe. Their courtship had been traditional yet modern: arranged by their families, but with plenty of time to get to know each other before the wedding. Those first years had been a dream of mutual understanding and shared hopes.

"Sarang!" she called, her voice a mixture of excitement and nervousness. "Can you come here?"

He walked into the kitchen, his work shirt slightly rumpled from a long day at the engineering firm where he worked. His eyes met hers, questioning.

Lavanya held out the test, a tentative smile spreading across her face. "We're going to have a baby."

For a moment, time seemed to suspend. Then Sarang's face transformed—first with shock, then with a broad, genuine smile that reached his eyes. He swept her into his arms, spinning her around. "We're going to be parents!" he exclaimed, his joy infectious.

Their families were equally thrilled. Lavanya's mother immediately began planning, talking about nursery colours and family traditions. Sarang's parents spoke of continuing the family line, their traditional expectations clear in their excited conversations. Aunts and cousins called with congratulations, each bringing their own unsolicited advice about pregnancy and childbirth.

"You must eat more ghee," one aunt insisted. "It will make the baby strong."

"Rest is important," another would add. "But don't become lazy."

The societal expectations were overwhelming, yet Lavanya felt a strange comfort in these age-old rituals. She was fulfilling her role—becoming a mother, completing the narrative her community had always anticipated for her.

Sarang seemed equally caught up in the excitement. He started reading parenting books, accompanied her to doctor's appointments, and spoke softly to her belly in the evenings. "Our little one," he would murmur, his hand gentle on her still-flat stomach.

But beneath the joy, Lavanya began noticing subtle changes. Sarang's mood would shift unexpectedly. A misplaced cup would trigger a sudden flash of irritation. When she suggested painting the nursery a soft yellow, his response was more aggressive than she expected.

"Why yellow?" he snapped. "Blue is better. For a boy."

The moment passed quickly. He would apologize, kiss her forehead, return to being the loving husband. But something felt different. A tension hummed beneath the surface, like a barely perceptible electrical current.

Her best friend, Meera, noticed it too. During a quiet coffee meetup, she watched Lavanya carefully. "Are you okay?" she asked. "You seem... different."

Lavanya brushed off the concern. "Just pregnancy hormones," she laughed. But the laugh didn't quite reach her eyes.

As her first trimester progressed, the tiny shifts in Sarang's behaviour became more pronounced. His control seemed to tighten imperceptibly—questioning her conversations, monitoring her phone, becoming increasingly possessive under the guise of protection.

"I just want to keep you and our baby safe," he would say, his hand squeezing her arm just a fraction too hard.

The dreams of motherhood remained vivid. Lavanya imagined holding her child, creating a world of love and safety. But a small voice in the back of her mind was beginning to whisper that something wasn't right.

As the chapter closed, the initial joy of pregnancy was subtly overshadowed by an emerging sense of unease—a foreboding that something was changing, something fundamental was shifting in their relationship.

The baby kicked. Lavanya placed her hand on her stomach, simultaneously filled with hope and a growing, inexplicable fear.

The metallic taste of fear began to settle into Lavanya's daily existence like an unwelcome guest. What had once been Sarang's occasional mood swings now transformed into a persistent storm of control and anger. Her pregnancy, which should have been a time of joy and anticipation, became a minefield of walking on eggshells.

It started subtly. Sarang began questioning her every move. Who had she spoken to? Why did she take so long at the grocery store? Why was she messaging her friend Anjali so frequently? His inquiries, initially disguised as concerned care, gradually morphed into invasive interrogations.

"You're pregnant," he would say, his voice tight with a strange mixture of possessiveness and threat. "You need to be more careful about who you interact with."

Lavanya tried to rationalize his behaviour. The stress of becoming a new father, the financial pressures, the societal expectations—she convinced herself these were driving his increasing volatility. Her mother's traditional advice echoed in her mind: "A good wife understands her husband's struggles and supports him."

But understanding was becoming increasingly difficult.

One evening, when Anjali called to check on her, Sarang snatched the phone mid-conversation. "She doesn't need to know everything about our life," he hissed after cutting the call. His eyes, once warm and loving, now burned with an intensity that made Lavanya's heart race.

Her world was shrinking. Invitations from friends went unanswered, her social media accounts became ghost towns, and family gatherings grew increasingly rare. Sarang's control extended beyond mere conversations—he managed their finances, decided her daily schedule, and monitored her movements with a precision that felt suffocating.

The physical changes of pregnancy made her more vulnerable. Her body was transforming, her emotions were heightened, and her usual confidence was being systematically eroded. Sarang seemed to sense this vulnerability and exploited it mercilessly.

"Who would want you now?" he would taunt during his anger episodes. "Pregnant and dependent on me. You should be grateful I'm still here."

These words, delivered with calculated cruelty, began to chip away at Lavanya's self-worth. The joyful woman who had celebrated her pregnancy just months ago was becoming a shadow of herself—anxious, withdrawn, perpetually on edge.

Her doctor, Dr. Mehra, noticed the changes during her routine check-ups. The bruises she carefully concealed with makeup, the tremor in her hands, the way she flinched when anyone moved too quickly—these were not just pregnancy nerves.

"Is everything okay at home, Lavanya?" Dr. Mehra asked gently during one consultation, her experienced eyes studying Lavanya's increasingly fragile demeanour.

Lavanya wanted to speak, to break the suffocating silence. But years of conditioning, of being told that family secrets must remain hidden, sealed her lips. "Everything's fine," she mumbled, avoiding direct eye contact.

But nothing was fine. The cracks in their relationship were no longer hairline fractures but gaping wounds. Sarang's untreated mental health issues were transforming their home into a psychological battlefield, and Lavanya was losing ground with each passing day.

Her best friend Anjali became her sole lifeline. Despite Sarang's attempts to isolate her, Anjali's persistent messages and occasional secret phone calls reminded Lavanya that a world existed beyond her current nightmare.

"Something's not right," Anjali would say. "I can hear it in your voice. If you need help, I'm here."

But admitting the truth felt impossible. The shame, the societal judgment, the fear of breaking her family's expectations—these were invisible chains holding her captive.

As her pregnancy progressed, the tension escalated. Small disagreements erupted into volcanic arguments. Sarang's temper became increasingly unpredictable, his control more suffocating. Lavanya began to realize that the man she had married was transforming into someone she no longer recognized.

The chapter closes with a sense of mounting dread. Something was coming—a confrontation, a breaking point—and Lavanya could feel it approaching with the inexorable certainty of a gathering storm.

Her unborn child kicked softly inside her, a gentle reminder of the life she was fighting to protect.

The sound of breaking glass shattered the silence, followed by Sarang's thunderous footsteps. Lavanya pressed herself against the wall, her hand instinctively protecting her swollen belly. Her breath came in short, terrified gasps as she realized this moment was different from all the others.

The pregnancy had transformed Sarang's controlling behaviour into something more sinister. What began as subtle manipulation had escalated into physical threats. Tonight, something inside him had finally broken.

"Where were you?" Sarang's voice was a low, dangerous growl. "I called you three times. Why didn't you answer?"

Lavanya's voice trembled. "I was at the doctor's routine check-up. I told you about this appointment weeks ago." Her mind raced, calculating the safest response, the way she had learned to do over these past months.

Sarang's eyes were wild, pupils dilated with a rage that terrified her. He grabbed her shoulders, his fingers digging into her flesh. "You're lying," he hissed. "You're always lying to me."

The next moments happened in a terrifying blur. His hands moved from her shoulders to her neck. Lavanya felt the pressure increasing, cutting off her air. The world started to spin, her vision blurring. Her unborn child—their child—was her only thought.

In that moment of absolute terror, something broke inside Lavanya. The fear transformed into a primal survival instinct. With a strength she didn't know she possessed, she managed to knee Sarang, catching him off guard. He stumbled back, momentarily stunned.

Gasping for air, Lavanya realized the brutal truth. This wasn't love. This wasn't a rough patch in their marriage. This was dangerous. This was life-threatening.

A compassionate nurse named Deepa, who had been concerned about Lavanya's previous visits, became her unexpected lifeline. During her last medical appointment, Deepa had quietly slipped her a card for a women's support centre.

"If you ever need help," Deepa had whispered, "this organization provides confidential support for women in challenging situations."

Now, trembling and bruised, Lavanya retrieved that card from her hidden drawer. Her fingers traced the contact information, a lifeline to potential freedom.

The support centre's counsellor, Anjali, listened carefully when Lavanya called. Her voice was calm, professional, yet compassionate. "You're not alone," she reassured Lavanya. "We can help you create a safe exit strategy."

They discussed practical steps: documenting the abuse, securing financial resources, finding temporary accommodation. Each conversation chipped away at Lavanya's fear, replacing it with a growing sense of determination.

Her family would be shocked. Society would have opinions. Her in-laws would undoubtedly pressure her to "adjust" and "save her marriage." But Lavanya's maternal instinct now burned brighter than her fear.

"I will not let my child grow up thinking this is normal," she whispered to herself, feeling her unborn child kick—almost as if in solidarity.

The decision crystallized: She would leave. Not tomorrow, not someday, but soon. Carefully. Strategically.

Lavanya began preparing discreetly. She gathered important documents, saved money in a separate account, and created a safety plan. Each small action was an act of resistance, of reclaiming her life and protecting her child's future.

As night fell, she looked at her reflection—bruised but unbroken. The woman staring back was no longer the naive, hopeful bride from just a few years ago. She was a mother, a survivor, preparing to fight for her child's safety and her own dignity.

The journey ahead would be challenging. But for the first time in years, Lavanya felt something she had almost forgotten—hope.

Her hand rested on her belly. "We're going to be okay," she whispered. "I promise."

The moonlight filtered through the curtains, casting a soft, protective glow—a silent witness to her transformation and her courage.

The morning sunlight filtered through the small window of Lavanya's new apartment, casting a warm glow on the carefully arranged space. It was modest but filled with hope - a stark contrast to the suffocating environment she had left behind. Her daughter, Aria, now three months old, slept peacefully in a portable crib, her tiny chest rising and falling with each breath.

Lavanya's journey hadn't been easy. After leaving Sarang, she had initially stayed with her parents, who had been nothing short of supportive. Her mother had held her during countless nights of tears, while her father had helped her navigate the legal complexities of separation. Her in-laws, contrary to her initial fears, had been understanding. They recognized Sarang's untreated mental health issues and supported Lavanya's decision to prioritize her and Aria's safety.

The therapy sessions had been transformative. Dr. Mehra, the counsellor she had first connected with through the women's support centre, had helped Lavanya understand that the abuse was not her fault. "You are not responsible for Sarang's actions," she would often remind Lavanya. "Your only responsibility is to protect yourself and your child."

Slowly, Lavanya began to rebuild her confidence. She had started working part-time as a freelance graphic designer, a skill she had always loved but had been discouraged from pursuing during her marriage. Her best friend Anjali had been instrumental in this process, helping her create an online portfolio and connecting her with potential clients.

Financial independence was crucial. Lavanya had meticulously documented the instances of abuse, which helped her secure temporary alimony and child support. More importantly, she was creating a life where she and Aria could thrive, not just survive.

The healing wasn't linear. Some days were harder than others. Triggers would emerge unexpectedly - a loud noise, a particular tone of voice, a memory. But each time, Lavanya was getting stronger. She was learning to recognize these moments, to breathe through them, to remind herself that she was safe.

Her relationship with Aria became her greatest source of strength. Every smile, every giggle was a reminder of why she had fought so hard. "We're going to be okay," she would whisper to her daughter during their quiet moments together. "More than okay."

The support network she had built was crucial. Her parents visited regularly, helping with Aria and providing emotional support. Her in-laws, despite their initial connection to Sarang, had been surprisingly supportive, acknowledging that Sarang's untreated mental health had been the root of their marital problems.

Lavanya had learned that Sarang was now receiving treatment. While she maintained strict boundaries, she hoped he would find the help he needed. Her decision to leave wasn't about revenge, but about creating a safe, healthy environment for herself and Aria.

As she watched her daughter sleep, Lavanya realized how much she had transformed. The woman who had once felt trapped, who had rationalized abuse and lived in constant fear, was now a confident, independent mother. She had reclaimed her narrative, her identity.

Her journey wasn't just about survival anymore. It was about thriving, about showing Aria what strength, resilience, and self-love looked like. Every small victory - a completed design project, a peaceful night's sleep, a moment of genuine happiness - was a testament to her journey.

The afternoon light began to soften, casting long shadows across the room. Aria stirred, her tiny hand reaching out. Lavanya picked her up, holding her close, feeling the warmth and promise of their shared future.

"We're home," she whispered. And for the first time in years, she truly meant it.

As the day drew to a close, Lavanya felt a sense of peace wash over her. She was no longer defined by her past, but by her resilience, her love for her daughter, and her unwavering hope for the future.

Epilogue

To err is human, to forgive is divine...
To fall is human, to rise is resilience...
Be a soul of resilience...
And rise like a phoenix...

www.ingramcontent.com/pod-product-compliance
Lightning Source LLC
LaVergne TN
LVHW041030150826
845672LV00001B/253
9798897240937